The Latest Version of My Love Story

Sean Boling

Published by Sean Boling, 2016.

This is a work of fiction. Similarities to real people, places, or events are entirely coincidental.

THE LATEST VERSION OF MY LOVE STORY

First edition. January 4, 2016.

Copyright © 2016 Sean Boling.

ISBN: 979-8224274895

Written by Sean Boling.

CHAPTER I

I listen to people talk.

Nobody is ever wrong.

The only time we admit to being wrong is when we talk about getting involved with the wrong people.

It only gets worse when we write. We've had time to think about our story, so we stick it full of meaning, then act like we knew what was going on the whole time we tell it.

I want to write about what happened, but don't want to sound smarter than I am.

Mom didn't dish out many words of wisdom. She didn't think of herself as that type. She worked so much retail, that by the time she switched to food service and looked the part of the wise-cracking waitress, it was too late. She was used to being agreeable. But she said something once that got my attention. She said Grace is the name of an angel that tells you when to say something nice, and when to shut up. It stuck with me because I'm good at saying nice things, but not shutting up. I figured my angel wasn't Grace. Mine was Gabby. So maybe I can write something worthwhile. Especially now that I've done some things that weren't so nice, even while I was still saying nice things the whole time.

The story I want to write is a love story, so that should help. That should keep me humble. We're willing to admit love baffles us. It's why we get involved with all those wrong people.

He wasn't a bad person. He wasn't that kind of wrong. He was a wonderful person, and probably even better now than he was then. I could say the timing was wrong, but the timing allowed us to meet, so that's not really true. I could say it wasn't meant to be, but we did love each other, so we were kind of meant for each other.

I can't think of the right cliché. That's why I want to write down my thoughts and stare at them. Maybe I'll see something as they stare back.

Maybe my search for meaning will change my memories. I took some psychology courses at our community college to train for my old job. I learned we're unreliable hosts of our past.

The moments seem clear to me, but in the way things are clear early in the morning, right before the sun rises. There is light, but everything is gray. I'd like to believe that putting them into words will be the sunrise.

Another thing I learned in psych class is that love is a chemical reaction. It's all in the mind. The heart has nothing to do with it. The heart is a muscle.

The creation of the universe was also presented as a chemical reaction.

But what lit the fuse?

My chemical reaction didn't even ignite for a while. I liked Cal well enough, but we were both married. Even more to the point, I was in a phase of life where I assumed those sparks had flown and popped. I was on my way to being a nurturer. A little earlier than expected, thanks to my forced retirement from the state hospital. My daughter was determined to stick with her high school sweetheart, and I figured a baby was the next logical step in her mind to try and make it work. She would be a little older than me when I had her. Meanwhile my stepdaughter was still only twelve. I was destined to sit and watch children do things. I was already overweight and often tired. I was well-prepared for what awaited me.

I remember the day when Cal and I decided there was a chance we could re-create the universe. It could just as easily have been our last day together.

He sat in his pickup truck across the street from the gated entrance. The gate was impressive. Red brick walls billowed out from each side, and a matching brick driveway rolled out from under it, like a tongue sticking out at all those who didn't live there. The exhibition made his truck look even more beaten up than it was, and his posture behind the wheel all the more slouched.

I wasn't that surprised to find him there. I pulled up next to him, facing the opposite direction so our windows were next to each other. His was already rolled down, and I smiled as I lowered my own. He didn't seem surprised to see me, either.

"Did you forget the code?" I asked.

He shook his head.

"Why don't you go in, then?"

"I picked up my stuff yesterday."

"So what are you doing here?"

He glared past me at the gate.

"Why did she have to cancel so suddenly?" he asked, though he didn't seem to be asking me.

I answered anyway.

"She has to leave. Has to sell her house."

"But she could have had one more class, so we could say goodbye. I've got a thing for saying goodbye to people."

"I get it," I said, and I really did. "But that's not how she is. You know that."

"I know."

"Her own daughter told us. Remember?"

"I remember."

"She said, 'mother provides, then provides little else.'"

"I was there."

"So what did you expect?"

"Couldn't she see we were different?" he kept his eyes on the gate. "We were so close."

"We still are. We don't need some last-day potluck."

"You and me, sure. But it's different with Laurie and Hannah."

I tried not to smile at hearing him single out our relationship. I wanted to keep a concerned expression on my face as he continued, in case he looked at me again.

"I would have liked a chance to talk to them some more," he said, still focused on the gate.

"You know where to find them."

"It's too awkward. I don't want to bother Laurie at work. And Hannah's even worse. Do I go into her parents' restaurant and chat her up? Half my age?"

"She's not half your age."

"She's underage. I'd feel like a pervert."

"We can throw a party of our own."

He shook his head and leaned back, shifting his gaze through the windshield.

"Too sad," he claimed.

"As sad as hanging around outside the gate?"

"I was going to use the pedestrian entrance, take a walk around the neighborhood. But I thought I might look suspicious."

"As opposed to lurking across the street?"

He smiled. That made me happy.

"In a dirty white pickup truck," I laid it on.

"At least it's not a van."

"That'll put their minds at ease."

I reached out my window. He looked at me and took my hand.

"Come in with me," I offered.

"Nah," he released his grip. "I'll wait."

"Promise?"

He rolled his eyes.

"Come on, Fina."

"I'm not worried you're going to do anything," I explained. "I just really want to have coffee with you."

"Okay, then."

"Be right back."

"I'll be lurking."

I taxied off the gray pavement onto the red brick driveway that led to the gate, and dialed the seven digits that made the iron bars swing slowly outward, as though giving you a long look before letting you in.

The neighborhood didn't quite live up to the splendor of its entrance, but still managed to look affluent. The lots were large enough to accommodate homes that came standard with three-car garages, and a more dense display of trees and shrubs than in the sparse countryside that spread out from the walls that surrounded the little empire. The front yards were bound together by lawns that extended down each side of every street. There were no sidewalks, only storm drains. It came across as a leafy Northeastern suburb that had been delivered to the high desert of the rural West.

The teacher's house had a detached studio in the backyard behind the garage. She mentioned more than once that no other home in the community had one. Her husband built it. He was a contractor who traveled the world to work on enormous projects, and she said that building something much smaller with his bare hands had been comforting for him. She told the story on the first night of class, as an introduction to why she liked to teach sewing, her point being that she also liked to make things by hand, and help others do the same.

I went around the side of the garage. There was no fence because the neighborhood was so safe, according to the teacher. A note was taped to the door of the studio:

Sorry I missed you, Fina. Come on in. It's unlocked.

Signed,

Joy

I had a feeling she would do that.

She insisted that we call her "Joy", but in my mind I always thought of her as "Joyce". It was a much better fit.

Inside the studio, things looked the same. It had only been a week since what turned out to be the final class, but I thought maybe she would have packed up some of the machines and furniture in anticipation of the move. The four sewing machines were still two to a side, the supply bins were still in the center, and the shelves lining the top of the room still held examples of past projects: pillows, swatches from quilts, pillows, scarves, pillows, knit hats, and more pillows.

I had an inkling she might be hiding in the house. I was tempted to look in the window along the top of the garage door and see if her car was there, but I wasn't that interested in embarrassing her.

We were all caught as unaware as she was when it came to how close we grew to one another. I would probably be the most likely to imagine things turning out the way they did, since I make an effort to flood my mind with positive thoughts ever since the assault. But I cannot pretend to make that claim. I figured it would be a pleasant enough class, but assumed that most people who wanted to learn how to sew wanted to learn how to be alone.

And at first that appeared to be the case.

Joyce certainly wasn't going to lead a "get to know each other" session on the first night of class. She greeted each of us at the door as we arrived and shuttled us to our stations. Her smile was broad, but her eyes didn't play along. Her smile said "I'm happy to be here" and her eyes said "Who, me?" She barely introduced herself before launching into an orientation on how to operate the sewing machines, which led immediately into our first project: making name tags for our supply cubbies.

But I felt weird not knowing any of the people in the room. My reasons for learning to sew were so personal, and I suspected the others also had interesting reasons for learning a craft that had long ago left home for work in the factories.

Cal was the most intriguing, since he was the only male in the course, and hardly looked like anyone's stereotype of a man drawn to such a hobby. He carried himself as if he was still muscular, in spite of that time having passed maybe a few years earlier. I wondered if he was going to bring in lots of camouflage fabric to work with, or maybe leather.

Hannah was the least likely of the women, according to my preconceptions, since she was so young. I had expected to be the young one in a room full of old ladies.

Laurie was around my age, but stood out in her own way. She seemed like neither arts nor crafts would interest her. I associated sewing with women who wore roomy chambray shirts that smelled like potpourri. Laurie instead came across as the owner of a sweat shop, who was learning how to sew in order to make sure the captives met their quotas.

Cal sat at the machine across the aisle from me, while Hannah was in the station in front of me. Laurie was at a diagonal, on the other side of the supply station where we would park our cubbies. So it was between Cal and Hannah for my first victim of conversation. Hannah was a bit closer to me, but would have to turn around to talk, so I went with Cal.

I had enough impulse control to wait until the time was right. When Joyce was hovering over Laurie, I checked my volume and leaned his way.

"I'm concentrating so hard on the stitching, I'm afraid I might misspell my name," I giggled.

He smiled and didn't say anything, but didn't appear to be wishing I'd shut up. Though I'm not a very good judge of that.

"Plus I'm using my full name," I continued. "And I never use it. I had to remind myself how to write it."

He looked over at my material, which was a relief. My stitches were halfway to the end of the name I'd written.

"Josefina?" he confirmed.

I nodded, proud of expressing myself non-verbally, if only for a moment.

"You go by Josie, then."

"Nope," I smiled. "Fina."

"Because everyone goes by Josie," he grinned.

"That's right."

He went back to concentrating on his name without sharing it with me.

"Cal," I read it aloud. "Short for Calvin?"

"Should I have gone with Vin?"

"People would take it for the wrong name."

"And it's not unique."

"I was twelve," I explained lightly. "I wasn't fitting in, so I figured I'd go full rebel."

"Rebels are temporary," he said.

I must have expressed myself non-verbally again, and very well, for he addressed my confusion before I could say anything.

"They find each other and form circles of their own, then fill them with other rebels."

And that was the end of our first conversation. I think he smiled politely as he swam away, but that's probably just the way I want to remember it.

I did take note of the way he sewed his name. Of that I'm certain. He had written it in big, block, capital letters, and was determined to fill the blank spaces with stitching, rather than just sew along the lines, which left him still stuck on the "C".

Joyce noticed as she walked by his station, and gave him some assistance on how to make quick turns that would cover the spaces in a way that looked more like a solid blob, rather than a bunch of zigging or parallel lines. She didn't appear to mind that we had been talking. Eventually we came to understand that she rarely appeared to notice anything that happened above the machines, and the first evening provided our first clue.

I left him alone for the rest of that first session. I liked to talk, but was a little better at controlling myself around a man. I was concerned about coming across as a spinster who was too enthusiastic about talking to one. When it came to women, on the other hand, I tended to let it rip. So after class I caught up with Hannah and Laurie as we walked to our cars and introduced myself.

I spun my introduction into an invitation to have coffee together the following week, our second class together.

There was a coffee house in the shopping center lining the freeway ramp that served as the access point on the journey to and from Joyce's gate. I asked the girls to join me there after class as we worked on our pillows. They were within reasonable earshot, to my front and my flank. Cal had positioned himself at the sewing station Laurie had occupied the previous week, on the other side of the supply cabinets, so I didn't get a chance to talk with him, much less invite him to coffee. I tried not to read too much into his move.

I had to chase him down to extend an invitation on our behalf as he climbed into his truck. He had taken off ahead of us the moment Joyce excused the class, and his station was closest to the door.

He declined, as I suspected he would, but I thought it might soften him up for next time, or sometime after that.

"Looks like it's just the three of us," I announced to Hannah and Laurie as I rejoined them in Joyce's driveway to confirm our plan. We bid each other farewell till our re-gathering in five minutes, and I realized I had left my purse in the studio in my rush to catch up to Cal.

Joyce was crossing the lawn toward her house when I flagged her down. She didn't break stride as she threw open her smile and told me the door was open.

After grabbing my purse from under the sewing table, I paused by the cubbies to admire everyone's names, our first project. Hannah's was cute, Laurie's was firm, and mine was curly. The first letter of Cal's was ragged, but the rest were filled in thoroughly thanks to the tips Joyce had given him.

A few sheets of paper sat in his box. I noticed them because they were from a yellow legal pad, rather than the crepe-like sewing pattern paper that rested in ours. His sheets were covered in scribbles, more than pattern paper could handle without tearing, and it appeared as though they weren't even drawings, but sentences. Some of them had been crossed out. I slid out one of the pieces and took a peek. I told myself it was simply to make sure he wasn't setting himself up for frustration by proceeding without a plan, or to learn a little something about him so that I could make him feel more welcome when I encouraged him to join us next time.

There were in fact no drawings, just words, and most of them were crossed out. The ones that survived were framed by all the ones buried under swipes of his pen. The survivors read like small poems. I figured he was going to sew them onto his pillows, but they didn't come across as the sorts of things you would find thrown onto a bed or a couch. One of them went something like this...

My arms turned into smoke
When I tried to hold her
They would float through her
And hide her from me

Some found some humor as they felt their way through the darkness...

You don't know
what I mean because
neither do I

But some were just plain dark...

Embrace the near
Kill the far
The history

of the world
in six words

Or something like that.

Laurie and Hannah, in that order, were driving through the gates as I caught sight of them. I figured the gates would close before I reached them, but they stayed open, apparently breaking down while we were in class.

Passing through those gates was like changing the channel from a fairy tale to a reality show. The plots of land were still pretty large, and people had built their dream homes on them, but their dreams were on a budget. Many of the houses weren't even built, they were delivered. They had random additions, mostly made of plywood, jutting out from one end or the other as more money or inspiration came in. Some parcels had dusty rose bushes lining the perimeter or the driveway, some had an old horse or a llama fenced in to one of the corners, but the most common feature was trampled ground, starting to turn hard as asphalt after the winter rains had moved on. Aside from an occasional oak tree or wispy landscaping tree planted by an owner who had neglected it since, the main plant life was weeds. They were enjoying a few weeks of being green before being choked yellow, and seeing them reminded me that my eyes and nose should be running.

I fought that trigger, resisted the urge to rub my eyes, but couldn't do much about the fogginess that rolled into my head most days every spring as the world started to bloom. I felt sharp enough when I talked or had a task to perform, but in quiet moments would feel the tide rise behind my face. When it was highest, I felt capable of agreeing to anything just to take my mind out of the froth. The world would seem to float past me without noticing I was there.

I nearly reached that point by the time I drove past the newer tract homes that rubbed against the strip mall by the freeway entrance. Hannah and Laurie were getting out of their cars as I pulled into the parking lot, which pushed my head above the fog line. It was show time.

I often imagine myself being interviewed on a talk show, even though I know that will never happen. It's a way for me to think through things, ask questions of myself and see what answers I come up with. I do the same when talking with others. But I conduct the interview, I stick to asking the questions. My parents taught me that people want to talk about themselves, and if you let them, they'll like you.

Daytime television was always being broadcast in the common areas when I was still on the job, which meant a lot of talk shows. Since I was always interested in why the patients were sentenced to our hospital, I would think of them as guests on my show, and ask questions in the same way I saw the hosts do it on the screens that surrounded us.

"You've always maintained your innocence. What is it about your condition that leads you to believe you bear no responsibility for what you did?"

"You claim to hear voices. Do they sound like anyone you know? Or are they the voices of strangers?"

"There has been a lot written about you, mostly by doctors. Is there something people would be surprised to know about you? Something that doesn't show up on the reports?"

And off they'd go, sometimes even after I had left the room. I'd pass by to check on them and they would still be talking, maybe even answering the question, if I could remember what it was.

So my appreciation for the talk show format bloomed.

I settled into it with Laurie and Hannah once we had our drinks in hand. The weather hovered between winter and spring, so drink temperatures could go either way. Hannah went with a hot coffee, Laurie iced.

"Neither of you fit the stereotype of a person in a sewing class," I said after each of our drinks had been announced and we stopped shuffling our chairs into position around the table. "So why is it you signed up for one?"

They looked at one another to see who would answer first.

"Hannah?" I suggested. "Why don't we start with you."

"What is the stereotype?" she asked back.

"Oh," I stalled, not used to people dodging an opportunity to talk about themselves. I almost asked Laurie if she'd like to get us started instead. "Well," I forged on, "I was thinking it would be women in fleece vests who know exactly how many cats are in their neighborhood."

They laughed, much to my relief. I was afraid for a second I may have come across as cruel.

"I was thinking a bunch of book club types," Hannah said.

"That's not the same thing?" Laurie asked.

"No," Hannah thought about it. "Wealthier women. The kind who donate money to charity but hate poor people."

"I thought there'd be a bunch of perfect mom types," Laurie said, "already good at all that other crap I suck at, like baking and gardening, and sewing would be their latest mom talent to rub my nose in, to prove to themselves how sad people are who don't have kids."

She seemed to regret how aggressive that sounded, and the table was hushed for a beat.

"Speaking of moms," Hannah came to her rescue, "that's really kind of why I'm here. My Mom never learned to speak English very well. She didn't have to. She was always in the back cooking in our restaurant..."

"Which one?" I jumped in. "I'm sorry. I get excited about food."

"That's okay," she assured me. "Best Pho."

"Ooh, I love pho," I said. "So what's it called?"

"Best Pho," Laurie helped her out. "You've never heard of it?"

"Dad's idea," Hannah added. "His English is only a little better than hers. I tried to tell him we were the only pho, at least until that place in the Oak Meadow Mall opened."

"Oh, so you're the one on Stillwater," I realized.

"That's us."

"I just thought the sign was saying it's the best pho, and there was some other name I didn't notice."

"And you ate there a lot?" Laurie asked.

"A fair amount," I shrugged.

"Ever meet anybody there?" she continued.

"Yes."

"Where did you tell them to meet you?"

"That Vietnamese place on Stillwater."

"Got a nice ring to it," Hannah joked, as Laurie seemed genuinely bothered by my ignorance.

"Thank you," I leaped on board her efforts to cover for me, then asked what sewing has to do with her mother.

"She loves it," she answered. "It's something we can do together that doesn't involve talking. My Vietnamese got pretty bad while I was going to school. Now we communicate like a couple of five-year olds."

"Sounds like me and my grandparents," I said. "But you're being much more sweet about it. I didn't try very hard to bond with them. I figured everyone's grandparents just kind of sat in the corner and smiled."

"I wish my grandparents didn't speak English," Laurie jumped in. "And my parents. I wish they all just sat in a corner and smiled."

She laughed, and it sounded kind of mean.

"Rough childhood?" I directed the interview her way.

"Loud," she said.

"I hear that," Hannah saw an opportunity to connect with Laurie. "Only in my case, the people are quiet and the kitchen equipment is loud."

"Listen to a lot of music?" Laurie asked her.

"Oh yeah."

"Headphones?"

"Well, earbuds."

"Of course. CD or cassette?"

Hannah giggled.

"I know, I know," Laurie said. "Digital."

She hunched over her drink and sucked a long sip of her iced coffee through the straw.

"Mom pretended headphones bothered her," she continued. "But I swear she enjoyed it. Gave her another excuse to yell. 'Can you hear me, Laurie? Hello! Hello! Can you hear me? Hello!'"

"So I imagine you do something quiet for a living," I said.

"Kind of," she nodded. "I run a wealth management company."

"Here?" I sounded as stunned as Hannah looked.

"Some big farmers and family money," Laurie shook her cup and rattled the ice cubes. "You'd be surprised."

"What does that have to do with sewing?" I followed up, like a good interviewer does.

"People can do what I do online, do it themselves."

"What, like investments and stuff?" Hannah asked.

"Yup."

"But that takes time," I said. "Right? They have to put in some effort, and study."

"Sure," Laurie agreed. "For now. But it's only going to get easier. Those algorithms big-time fund managers use, the kind that trade automatically by the split second? They'll work their way down to us. Technology never stays on its leash."

"And sewing is the answer?" I kept the interview focused.

"Being personable is the answer," she said. "Making gifts, offering a down-home feel. The kind of stuff I gag on."

"Do people really want their money manager to be down-home?" Hannah asked.

"Yeah," I added. "Don't they want someone who's all business and professional?"

"Business websites are professional. Humans need to be more human than ever. You can't beat a computer at its own game. So it's pot holders and cupcakes from here on out. Fuck."

Hannah and I stifled giggles, but Laure smiled to let us know it wasn't necessary to hold back.

"You don't have to be someone you're not to be more human," I claimed.

"If my clients want someone who acts like a man, they can hire one."

"How did you get their business in the first place?" Hannah asked.

"There wasn't much competition. The town wasn't much smaller, but the world was at a distance. My clients are getting old, and their kids are taking over. They don't settle for anything. Ever. Looking for satisfaction is what satisfies them."

"Kids these days," Hannah sighed mockingly, rolling her eyes on behalf of all young people.

I pretended Hannah didn't say anything and remained attentive to Laurie, who looked ready to fight back under the flag of older people everywhere.

"You can buy those things," I reminded her. "Those knick-knacks."

Laurie understood what I was doing, chuckled, and lowered her flag.

"Too expensive," she shook her head.

"You're already cutting back?" Hannah asked, ready to do her part to keep the peace.

Laurie shook her head again.

"Too cheap," she admitted.

We didn't restrain ourselves that time. We laughed in her face, and she loved it. We spent the rest of our first evening together confirming our comfort with one another. Even the spats ended up being fun. We could see the person we were disagreeing with, and we liked that person. Nothing was personal because everything was.

Every so often I would look at someone who wasn't talking, and as she listened to the others, she would look so grateful, as if saying a prayer without realizing she was saying it, silently giving thanks to have lucked into such an easy link.

It would have been easy to keep it at three, and not risk upsetting the exciting calm we were riding, but we decided to keep trying for that fourth member of our class.

I'd like to say there was something intriguing about Cal that motivated us, but I'm pretty sure we were just being polite. He seemed so out of place, and we had learned that first night how out of place we all felt.

CHAPTER II

My daughter didn't like it when I visited her at work. I thought where she worked was interesting, so I visited anyway. Usually I brought lunch.

She didn't think it was interesting, since she was the one who had to sit there for eight hours and make sure no alarms went off and no one climbed the fence and took a bat or a hammer to any of the solar panels.

There were thousands of them spread across a flat, treeless part of the valley floor that was like a desert, but with grass that never stayed green more than a few days a year.

"Why would anyone attack a solar panel?" I asked as I looked out the window from her office at the miles of shimmering rows. I always imagined they were contacting alien life.

"They really love coal?" Cheyenne kidded.

I named her Cheyenne because I was a teenager when she was born.

"Maybe they're from the windmill farm over the hill," I offered.

"Green energy cage match!"

She liked the idea, raising her fists as if promoting the fight. Then she shrugged.

"People just like to break things," she said. "Which is good for me, because that's the only reason I have a job. They can monitor the instruments from wherever they want."

"Why don't they build a higher fence?"

"Somebody cuts through it, digs under it, they need a witness."

"They can put in cameras."

"Are you trying to get me laid off?"

"Just thinking out loud."

"Your favorite thing to do."

"I like getting feedback on my thoughts."

"The investors feel better knowing there's a person on site."

"Even if it costs more?"

"They promised 300 jobs when they built this place. Turns out almost all of them were construction. When it was done, they had to keep a few people around for PR."

I stared out at the panels and thought of the signals pulsing through the shiny landscape, the energy being captured by them, the electricity monitoring them, the journey through the lines to places we couldn't see.

"It's been about five minutes since you got here," Cheyenne said. "Shouldn't you be talking about Augie by now?"

"That's not what I was thinking about."

"I didn't think you were thinking about anything. You were so quiet."

I smiled at her.

"I really don't mind Augie. I just don't think you should have a child with him."

"How is that not liking him?"

"I have no opinion of him. How could I? He's just there."

"He's low maintenance."

"So is the chair you're sitting in."

"Laughter, laughter."

"I'll bet that chair can go decades without any problems."

"Unlike Dad," she jabbed. "Where is he these days, exactly?"

I shrugged, arms wide, utterly past getting upset over the subject.

"He was exciting, though," Cheyenne said.

"He was," I agreed. "But I ain't singing that song from Dreamgirls over him. He ain't worth it. The one Jennifer Hudson belts out. What's it called?"

"I forget," she grinned. "The one that girls scream out on YouTube to show what a good singer they are. And young gay guys."

"That's the one. They sing it and they have no life experience. They don't know what it means."

"But you know what it means," she goaded me on. "Don't you, Mom?"

"Oh, I know, girl," I took her up on it. "Mm, mm, don't I know."

I started singing it as best I could remember. We took turns imitating some poor girl overestimating her talent. Cheyenne didn't even use any words. She would just scream. After my last turn, the one where I couldn't think of any more lyrics to make up, and my voice sounded even worse than when I started, after my daughter laughed at me, I tried to put a bow on the subject.

"I know I settled, too," I admitted. "Just later on in life. Mike's a nice guy. Not much of a pulse..."

Cheyenne nodded in agreement and bulged her eyes. Her nods and her eyes were too big. They were big enough to bother me. I wanted to strike back.

"But he's kind," I said. "Mike is quiet and low maintenance, but there's someone there. I don't see anything going on behind Augie's eyes. He still seems so interested in looking cool, and he's getting too old for that."

Not that he was old, but I knew very well how trying hard to be cool can age a person. Our conversation, on the other hand, was turning back time. I was driving Cheyenne back to the same kind of sullen mood she would get in as a teenager, when we first fought about Augie. I should have dropped the subject after our little singing contest.

"He's a lot like me, in a way," I backed off. "He says what's on his mind. There's just never anything on his mind."

Cheyenne was laughing again, even though I was insulting the love of her life. She was confident enough, and I had poked fun at myself enough to make it work. Maybe I wasn't such a bad parent. I beamed as brightly as the panels that stretched into the distance.

I thought of Cal's silence, and how different it was from Augie's, or Mike's. Cal was like the equipment that caught the light. He was quiet, but it was clear something was humming between the panes. There was energy and information surging through.

I brought him to the solar farm one day.

I introduced him to Cheyenne as a friend, which was still true at the time. I think I wanted her opinion of him, in case there was a chance. In spite of her commitment to her first and only lousy boyfriend, she was good at girl talk, at least to me. I never expect to accomplish much from those talks. All I want is humor and anger, and she was good at both.

Cal asked if we could walk through the farm, out amongst the solar panels. I don't think anyone had ever asked Cheyenne for permission, and I don't think she had ever done it herself.

"Want to come with us?" I asked her.

"Why?" she was baffled.

"To get out of the office."

"My only job requirement is to stay inside it."

"Suit yourself. Thanks for allowing us."

"Careful out there," she warned us. "The repairmen tell me it can be like a hall of mirrors if you don't know where you're going."

Each row did look like the others, and there were so many of them, in such a vast area, and it was all so quiet. It felt like something that had been abandoned thousands of years ago. But it was new, and so many people relied on it to make their lives comfortable. Thousands of people, maybe hundreds of thousands. Cheyenne told me the number once, but I forgot.

And it didn't need any of their help.

A hard wind blew through the gaps, but we were warmed by the sunlight being absorbed all around us. We would spend about ten minutes walking down a row. When we reached the end and turned up an aisle to the next row, the wind would bite us until we were snug between the next line of panels.

That was the day Cal and I started our "Robot or Not" game. It was something I had thought of playing with my husband Mike after his old job was lost to technology, but I realized he probably wouldn't be into it.

Cal and I would see someone doing their job, either helping us or another customer while we watched. We would look at each other when it was safe to talk and one of us would say, "Robot or not?" And we would decide if their job was going to be replaced by a machine someday. We started with our own jobs that day in the solar farm. Mine first.

We agreed that patients could get their meds easily enough through a machine.

"Patients?" Cal asked. "That's what you call them?"

"That's what the state calls them."

"Ever cure anyone?"

I pretended he didn't ask.

We agreed that cameras could keep an eye on them, but that they still needed a human presence.

"Especially if they need to be taken down," Cal kidded. Kind of.

"We could just gas them," I suggested.

"Listen to you," he teased.

"With a tranquilizer," I explained.

"That's not as fun," he kept it up.

Which led us into his old job.

"If you watch science fiction, then yes," he said. "Soldiers in the future will be robots."

"You don't think it's true," I could tell.

He shook his head and touched a panel to see if it was hot.

It was. I giggled at him.

"What about drones?" I returned to the topic. "Aren't we already heading there?"

"People like killing each other too much."

I probably giggled again, but more nervously, or said something like "oh, really?" in some overblown way.

Whatever it was, it was filler, a way to stall. I didn't know how to ask what I wanted to ask, which created an uncomfortable silence made deeper by the sound of the wind whistling past the panels.

Cal had some suspicions about what was on my mind.

"I didn't like killing people," he said.

"I'm not sure that's quite what I was thinking."

"Did it make me sad?" he tried again.

"Something like that."

"Is it why I've got problems?"

"That's probably about right."

"It didn't help. But the killing isn't what really got me."

"No?"

"Getting someone else killed. That's what did it."

"Really...?"

"Don't even try."

"What?"

"That's as much as you're getting out of me."

"But I'm good at this."

"Because you worked with the criminally insane?"

"Well..."

He smirked before I did.

I finished the punchline we had built together.

"...Yes."

We turned a corner, taking a face full of wind, and reversed course down the next aisle.

"Besides," he said once we were shielded by the equipment, "I'm not even sure what happened anymore. I went to lots of group therapy. We told our stories, and they were terrible. I started changing mine to keep up with the others. I don't know if I tried to make it less terrible, or more. But I know I made some changes, little ones each time I told it.

And I didn't even remember the story very well to begin with. So much of what I did on my tours was so boring. Driving for hours, walking for hours, sitting for hours, for days, for weeks, for months, and then all of a sudden the most intense moment of my life happens. How can I possibly remember a story like that? It's in a thousand pieces that won't hold still."

I always told my story to anyone who would listen, usually my therapist. She was the one who got me started. She had me tell it every session. She wanted me to own it, make it mundane, just another thing I talk about, like rain or how comfortable my shoes are. But telling it to Cal at that time would have felt like barter, as if I was only doing it so that he would return the favor. That's what he would be thinking about as he barely listened to me. So I decided not to share my story until he asked. I wanted him to care.

Maybe I wanted to get my story straight, too. He got me thinking about how much I may have changed it. I was pretty sure it had remained the same. My therapist would have called me out if she noticed any editing. If she was listening. I assumed she was listening.

Cal was capable of remembering things quite well when he wanted to. He remembered scenes from movies like a human video recorder. Not that remembering movies is anything like remembering our lives. A movie holds still. The same things happen every time. Especially the movies he liked. He wasn't into movies that might change along with you, the kind that can reveal a message you can stitch together if you want to try. He only watched romantic comedies. He had seen hardly any before going away to fight. Since he came back, he had seen nothing else.

None of us ever asked him if he was a veteran. He never made an announcement. It just became part of the conversation.

The movies are what helped him blend in when he finally agreed to join us after a few weeks of invitations. I'm sure he came along just so he could say that he did, and he could decline us in good conscience in the future. But we fit into his recovery program perfectly. He designed it himself. It was a regimen of fru fru to put his trauma behind him. The romantic comedies were a big part of it.

He had seen them all. Classics, terrible ones, underrated ones that never made it to a movie theatre and went straight to video. He watched the Hallmark Channel. He could quote from Twenty Seven Dresses as well as When Harry Met Sally. He could have drawn a comic book from memory based on Roman Holiday. He introduced us to rom coms from other countries.

"I've had it with men," he said toward the end of his first night out with us. He chugged the last swig of coffee from his cup now that it was cool enough, while the rest of us tried to process his announcement.

"Chasing Amy?" Hannah finally offered.

"What?" Cal chuckled.

"Is that a line from the movie Chasing Amy?"

"No," I disagreed. "It's from that one with Queen Latifah."

"She's been in, like, five," said Hannah.

"A feel-good movie is not the same as a romantic comedy," I countered.

"I've had it with men?" Laurie repeated Cal's line. "That's from every rom com ever made."

Cal seemed to have gotten high off his coffee, or off the camaraderie of a group who shared his interests. He slammed his empty cup onto the table as though he had just taken a shot of tequila in a bar and was about to scream something about partying.

"The only movies I want to see are romantic comedies," he growled. "The only animals I want to handle are cats and small dogs, and after I learn to sew, I'm going to sign up for a ceramics class. And I want to hang out with women. Just hang out."

"Then why didn't you come out with us before?" I asked. "I almost stopped asking."

"I'm still getting used to it," he said. "Like when you first start drinking beer. Plus I had a bad experience with the first group I tried."

"Who were they?" Hannah asked.

"A writing workshop," he shuddered.

I thought of the poems stuffed in his cubby hole back at the sewing studio. He had started to stitch one of them onto a pillow cover.

"They wanted me to write down war stories," he explained. "I'd say no, and they'd insist. 'Even if they're not yours,' they'd say, or 'You can write yours and change the names, play with the facts.' They wouldn't stop."

"Women," Laurie muttered.

Cal laughed along with the rest of us. I must have laughed the loudest.

"At least you got a poem out of it to stitch onto your pillow," I said, careful not to reveal that I had seen more than one of his poems.

"You noticed, huh?" he asked.

"I have a hard time keeping my eyes on my own work."

"How do you know I wrote it?"

He seemed to be tensing up.

"I don't. But you mentioned the workshop..."

He smiled to let me know he was messing with me.

"I wrote it," he admitted. "And I've got a bunch more."

"So it wasn't a total waste," Hannah jumped in.

"I'm putting them on pillows as a joke. They're these dark things I wrote to get those ladies off my back. I thought stitching them onto a poofy pillow would be funny. Maybe I can start a business. Ironic throw pillows."

"Or maybe they represent what you're trying to accomplish," I said.

"What do you mean?" he asked.

"You know," I tried to think of what I meant, "burying your past in a pillow."

That was too literal. I hardly got any reaction. I tried again.

"Your past is being cushioned by your new interests."

That was better. I earned some smiles, including one from Cal.

"You really like all those frilly things?" Laurie asked him.

"I don't have a choice," he grinned. "I need to like them."

His mouth remained in the same position, but it started to feel less like a grin. The smile had been drained from it.

We all seemed to notice, and each of us responded by contributing a version of "it's getting late, it's time to go home, let's do this again" as we gathered our belongings before dumping our cups in the waste basket on the way out.

Before our pack broke up in the parking lot, Hannah and Laurie and I exchanged hugs while Cal watched. Hannah shook his hand, as did Laurie, but I decided to try for a hug. He went with it, but while it was happening, I wished I had waited at least another week.

His vehicle and mine were next to each other, so I was stuck in awkwardness that much longer. Hannah and Laurie pulled out and waved to us while I mishandled my keys. Cal was still outside of his truck, and he wasn't trying to open his door. I focused on my keys, but could tell he was standing there, looking over his hood in my direction.

"Why so loud?" he asked.

"I have a lot of keys."

"I mean you," he came around to the row I stood in, where I faced my door.

"Me?"

"You talk so much."

I laughed, then quickly switched to a soft giggle.

"That's not the same as being loud," I said.

"The volume builds. And you gesture really big. Like someone is watching. Like you're performing."

"Is that a problem?" I asked, hanging the keys from my index finger and jangling them.

"I was just wondering why."

I almost said something dramatic, like "it keeps the demons away." But I didn't want to remind him of those women in the writing workshop.

"It's the way I was raised," I lied.

"Why would someone raise you that way?"

"So...it is a problem."

Which sounded more defensive than I felt. I just wanted to move past my lie, not expand on it.

"No," he explained. "It's not a problem."

"Good."

"I want to make sure it's not because you think that's the only way people will pay attention to you."

A warmth spread through my body and reached my hands. The keys hung silently. I was inspired to push my lie over the edge.

"Childhood was fine," I confessed. "Adulthood was the problem."

He appreciated the honesty.

"Too bad," he deadpanned. "It would be a lot easier to blame your parents."

"It's never too late to try," I played along.

"At least you're not fast," he said.

I wasn't trying to flirt. I'm such a lousy self-monitor. I almost grunted from shame.

"Talking loud and fast is a brutal combination," he explained.

I was relieved he was still talking about the way I talk. I hoped I didn't look relieved.

"One or the other is bearable," he continued. "And if you have to choose one, you've got the better of the two. I'll take loud over fast. Easier to imagine getting a word in."

"Someone you can talk to on the phone," I chimed in. "Not just listen to."

He smiled.

But once again whatever was behind it dissolved, and left behind the fossil of a smile.

"People used to notice me and I never had to say a word," he said. "Now I need to say something if I want to be seen, and I'm not used to it."

That would have been a good moment to tell him the story that I don't mind telling, but don't want to think about when I'm not telling it. The reason I build walls of sound with my voice. But it was the first night. I didn't want to scare him away.

Which was a better excuse than the one I was giving myself at the solar farm.

As we found ourselves in what seemed to be the center aisle of the solar panels, I wondered if I was growing more protective of my story. The path led straight toward the main office where Cheyenne sat somewhere behind the windows that threw a glare at us from the sun. We were a couple of dozen rows away, debating whether it was time to head back.

I told my tale so well, but hadn't thought of it as a tale until I met Cal. I didn't want to know if there were any cracks in it. Vowing not to tell him until he asked may prove that he cared, but I figured he never would. That's not the kind of talking he liked to practice.

Cal shielded his eyes from the windows' reflection and looked down the aisle.

"Is that your daughter?" he asked.

I squinted along with him and saw a figure walking our way through the heat that jiggled the air.

"No," I concluded. "That's not her stride."

We kept our eyes on the walker. It was like discovering a fellow survivor on a scorched earth.

Several steps closer, it became a man.

Several more, and he became a repairman. He had tools dangling on all sides of him.

"I hope we didn't get Cheyenne in trouble," I mumbled.

Faint clinking sounds reached our ears from the tools as they bounced in step.

Cal waved.

The repairman waved back.

I was going to say it was a good sign, but when I turned to say so, Cal was breathing heavily and shaking. He was sweating too, but so was I, thanks to the heat. It wasn't hard to imagine he was sweating harder than before, though.

"Are you okay?" I asked.

He didn't respond. He kept watching the repairman.

"She'll be fine," he finally said.

"I know," I assured him.

He was trying to calm himself down. Whatever he was trying wasn't working. There were some techniques I learned at the hospital that I considered suggesting, but decided to wait as long as possible. I was sure he would prefer to get through it on his own.

I kept looking back and forth between him and the repairman. I wanted to see if Cal was getting worse or better as the cause drew closer.

The repairman took a sharp turn down a row that was about a hundred yards in front of us. As soon as the vision was gone, Cal's breathing and shaking started to slow. He bent over with his hands on his knees. I waited until he stood up straight to ask him a question.

"Robot or not?"

"The repairman?" Cal asked.

"Yup."

"Eh," he looked around. "Maybe robot. But the terrain is rough. Lots of rocks it could trip over."

"Maybe one that hovers, then."

Cal looked at me for the first time since making it through the attack.

"A drone?" he smiled.

I nodded.

"Or do we like repairing things too much?" I asked.

"We might," he took a deep breath. "We just might."

CHAPTER III

Most twelve-year old girls who dye their hair purple do it to rebel, or assert their independence, or see what they look like with purple hair.

My stepdaughter did it to hide the gray.

Zola was already an anxious child by the time I met her. She was seven. Mike brought her to a lunch date after we had been seeing each other for a month. The restaurant had a children's menu with a picture on it to color. The hostess brought crayons to the table. Zola colored the whole page black.

Mike told me she had been a happy child until her mother disappeared. They had a running argument over whether she was abducted or she ran away.

"Dad didn't notice how unhappy she was," she would tell me.

"You were so young when it happened," I would say. "How could you remember that?"

"It was obvious."

"The police say she was kidnapped."

"Dad says the police say she was kidnapped."

"It's in the report."

"They were being nice," she always insisted. "People are nice to Dad. They would rather leave than be mean to him."

"I'm not going anywhere," I always assured her.

"People are supposed to say that."

"I mean it."

"I'm sure you do right now. That doesn't make it true."

Then, depending on my self-confidence in the moment, I would either sigh, laugh, or laugh then cry once I was out of her sight.

I stopped asking her to come to church with me around the time she turned ten. The last time she went with me she wore one of her homemade t-shirts. It was the white one she had written on with a thick black Sharpie, "My Mother Is A Missing Person".

Mike never went because he drove on Sundays. He drove a bus for a retirement community. He used to drive a bus for the county, but the service had too few buses for too large an area to be reliable, and it shrank to almost nothing once people started using the web to hire each other for rides. Mentor Manor was a pretty safe gig for a bus driver. The residents weren't interested in hiring strangers over the phone for anything, and few of their family members came to drive them. I told Mike that by the time driverless vehicles become common, he would be long gone, so he had nothing to worry about.

Sundays were a big day for the Manor. Lots of group field trips to concerts or ball games or museums in some of the larger cities a couple hours away.

I was tired of going to church alone. Before asking Cal to come with me, I remember asking Zola for the first time in a couple of years, just to see what would happen. Summer vacation was starting and I was hoping to get her out of the house, out of her room.

"That's all," I assured her. "Not because I expect you to be touched by the spirit or anything."

"It's full of old people," she said, reclined on her bed, on top of the sheets. It was hard to tell the difference between her clothes and her pajamas.

"Well, you don't seem to get along with young people."

"But the church people are really old. Their average age is, like, dead."

"Maybe there's a place full of middle-aged people I can take you."

"I'm fine, Fina. I have friends. They just don't live around here."

"They live online."

"They're real people," she sighed. "They live in New Hampshire, and Hawaii, and Latvia. And they like what I like. I don't know what to talk about with people around here."

"So you only want to talk about things you like?"

"I'm sorry," she sat upright and raised her voice. "I can't bounce around and smile and giggle like an idiot."

"Nobody's asking you to do that," I said, trying not to take what she described personally. "But maybe you can act like you don't hate people. Maybe we can start there. Start small."

When that didn't work, I turned to Cal for some company. I thought it might be too soon. The class had started in March, and he didn't come out with us until April. But I also thought it might be a good way to get him out of his room, too. He seemed to be deep into patterns. As far as I could tell, the sewing class was the only time he left his house.

He told us he lived in that big, weird house across from the water treatment plant, and we all knew what he was talking about. It was on a beleaguered patch of land that formed a triangle where a busy country road started to veer away from the railroad tracks. A yard full of weeds and scrub brush was at the tip of the fork, and the house took up the space where the plot fanned out. I saw his truck in the driveway one day not long after he told us, and I wondered how anyone ever backed out onto that road without getting sideswiped. The traffic wasn't all that heavy, but it was fast.

Imagining him in that house made me sad. It was way too big for one person. Most of the tenants I had seen living there before him were families. I remembered flashes of toddlers in pull-up diapers and matted hair making their way through the weeds. Cal had mentioned being separated from his wife and daughter. Hannah asked how old his daughter was. When he said six, Hannah and I said "aww" (as in "how cute") and then felt really stupid. Laurie apologized for us, and we didn't defend ourselves.

It looked like a huge playhouse. It was so basic, a rectangle that seemed to be made out of plywood, with no insulation, and windows that appeared to rattle with every vehicle that zipped by at highway speeds. I wondered how it could withstand a passing train. I couldn't imagine the inside was any more encouraging.

He said he lived there because he needed room. He wanted space between him and anyone who entered, so he could hear their footsteps before they reached him late at night. And during the day, he liked the noise and the vibration of the cars and trains, because daytime silence made him nervous. It was the kind of silence that waits to be broken.

Imagining him in that house also made me happy when he accepted my invitations. Any time spent with me was less time in those bare rooms that shook during the day, and echoed with footsteps that weren't really there at night.

His reaction to church surprised me. He said "sure" without hesitation or appreciation, as though I had asked him if he wanted a side of ranch dressing with his fries. I offered to drive to sweeten the deal.

"I have been neither damaged nor inspired by the church," he explained later as we ate cookies and sipped coffee in the fellowship hall after the service.

"Is that a quote from someone?"

"Me."

"It sounds like you've said it a lot," I said.

"When you've been to war, people like to ask you about God."

"I heard there are no atheists in a foxhole."

"There are no foxholes."

"You know what I mean."

"It goes both ways," he said. "Some find God, some lose God."

"Ah," I hadn't really thought of that before. "So there's 'God help me,' and there's 'God why has thou forsaken me?'"

"Do you think people ever talked like that?"

"With the 'thee' and the 'thou'?"

"I'll bet those words have been written a lot more than they've been spoken."

"Romantic comedies only lead up to the kiss," he explained. "I need to keep a hand in what happens after the closing credits."

"Real life stuff."

"Real life stuff that's not too stressful. And it gives me an honest answer for when people ask me what I do."

"You don't like to tell people you're a veteran."

"I don't want that to define me."

"Is it such a bad thing to be defined by?"

"It's a big thing, and it doesn't leave room for much else in people's minds."

Another old well-wisher advanced.

"Here, watch..." Cal said before she reached us. "Mention my service this time when you introduce me."

"Hello, Marjorie," I said as she arrived. "This is my friend, Cal."

"Hello, Cal," she shook his hand with the same posture full of pity that was all the rage that morning.

"Cal fought overseas," I told her.

"Really?" she stiffened up, as though she had just been pulled over by the police.

"Three tours," Cal added.

"Oh my."

Marjorie didn't appear to have any answers for the questions the imaginary officer was asking.

"Thank you for your service," she finally said.

She started to shake his hand again, but realized she already had, and went with a short bow instead.

"You're welcome, Marjorie," Cal said graciously, letting her know she was excused.

We watched her walk back to the lingering cluster.

"Let's go," he said without turning my way. "Before they start saluting me."

When we reached my car, he asked if we could go to Costco.

Which was fine with me, but I was half-expecting a horde of old folks to burst through the doors of the fellowship hall and stagger toward us like a horde of zombies moaning, "Thank you for your service."

"You sure it's okay?" he asked.

"Of course," I snapped out of my mild trance.

"I told you," he read my mind. "Say the magic words, and presto! I change from a person into a bald eagle."

The Costco was the tallest building for miles around, tied with the Home Depot and the Target. I parked in one of the more distant spaces because there were strange divisions between the lots that I could never figure out. I would see a good spot and suddenly come upon a cement planter box full of rosemary blocking my way. Cal didn't seem to mind being far away. He may have understood.

"What do you need?" I asked as we hiked into the more congested area near the front of the store.

"Nothing."

"Why are we here?"

"To catch the second service," he grinned.

I wasn't sure what he meant.

"This is my place of worship," he explained. "On the day of rest, I go to the day of samples."

We walked past the carts and he flashed his membership card to the vest on duty.

"Shouldn't we get a cart?" I asked. "At least pretend we're shopping?"

"Who do you think cares more about that? You or them?"

"Probably me."

"Definitely you."

He led me through the electronics section and made the turn toward some food.

"Come on," he beckoned. "It's like communion, but with a bigger variety of crackers."

"With stuff on top of them."

"That's right," he chuckled. "All kinds of stuff."

At some point during our stay at each tasting station, I would ask to see the box that the product came in. There was something very specific I was looking for. After hitting a few stations, Cal asked me what it was.

"Where it came from," I answered.

"The address of the company?"

"I like to check if I'm familiar with the city," I nodded. "And if I'm not, I look it up later."

"Why?"

"Because looking it up right there on the spot would look weird," I imitated someone tapping madly on their phone. "Like I'm obsessing over something."

"And you're clearly not," he smirked.

"I like to place things," I revealed. "I like to know where things are."

I was prepared to explain why that was, but he didn't follow up, as if he knew it involved the story of my last day at the state hospital. Instead, he gestured toward the next station as though we were on a ship and he had spotted land.

After we ate the stuffed mushroom caps that were offered to us, he started a game of "Robot or Not?"

"Tasting station workers," he said. "Robot or Not?"

"I'm not sure stores will be around," I said. "Much less their employees."

"Everything will be online?" he asked.

The word 'everything' got me thinking.

"Maybe not," I reconsidered. "Not when it comes to food."

"Where would we sample?" he gestured around the big box we were in.

"3-D printers?" I offered.

"No taste," he said. "It will only look like food."

"That's what these places will become," I decided. "Sampling stations."

"Food only. We'll try things, then touch a screen to order them."

"And they'll be delivered to our doorstep before we even get home."

"So we're back to the original question," he reminded me.

"Robot or not?" I verified.

"Do we need people to hand us the samples?"

"Yes."

"Why?"

"Eating needs company."

"We'll be surrounded by other people sampling."

"Who's going to spread the artichoke dip on the cracker?"

"A robot can't do that?"

"It's tricky," I claimed. "Lots of little movements."

"Then a machine will plop it on. The crackers will be on a conveyor belt. Will anyone care?"

"I think you want the robots to take over," I teased him.

"It doesn't matter what I want. It's happening."

"I think you are a robot."

"I can prove I'm not," he played along. "I'll pass your spread test. Give me some peanut butter, some saltines, and a knife. I'll even swirl some designs into it."

We came upon the next station that had some kind of crab salad on top of little hard pieces of bread. He joked around with the woman in the hair net who was putting them on display, wondering why she didn't put more flair into her presentation. She wasn't in on what we had been talking about, but was a good sport, and seemed to appreciate somebody noticing her.

Then Cal grew quiet. It was the kind of transition that happened often. I was getting used to it. His bounciness would last about as long as someone can hop on one foot.

"I was actually raised pretty religious," he said as we wandered away from the heavy traffic and food stations of the center aisle into an uninhabited one filled with office supplies.

I didn't even have to imagine I was interviewing him. He was starting to tell me things without any prompting. I gave him space.

"By my grandmother," he continued. "She would take me to her church on Sundays since my parents worked retail and restaurant jobs and didn't get many weekends off. And man, that was some church."

"How so?"

"Intense."

"Snake handlers?"

He smiled a little bit, which made me smile a lot.

"No," he said. "But they had this room. It was supposed to be some sort of heaven simulator. We would lie on the floor and a nice lady with a soothing voice would tell us to imagine a relaxing place and to fill it with loving people. She would give us time to imagine each part, and when we reached peak relaxation, when she was sure we were all settled down and soothed and not thinking of anything other than the beautiful place we were imagining and the loving people there with us, she'd tell us that's what heaven's like. And it sounded good. To a point. But I couldn't help but wonder if that's all there was, it would get pretty boring."

I laughed, but he didn't, so I cut it short.

"By that definition," he continued, "I'm in heaven on earth already. I've got the soothing place and little to do other than things I enjoy. Or maybe I'm seeing the future, when robots do all the work no one wants to."

"What about the loving people in the room with you?" I asked, then realized I should have had a more heated debate in my mind about whether to ask that question. I slowed my breathing to counter the jump in my heart rate.

He answered quickly, as though he had already thought of that part.

"It's all about relaxing," he said. "Whatever makes you happy."

"Your wife and daughter don't make you happy?" I asked, once again ignoring any questions I had about the question.

But he once again took it in stride.

"Let me show you something," he said, and beckoned me to follow him.

We backtracked to the electronics area. I caught up with him at a computer that was on display atop a bunch of boxes with the same type of machine inside them.

He went online and called up a video with the title "I Dare You To Watch This Without Crying."

A little girl sits in what looks like a pre-school or Kindergarten classroom and a teacher's voice in the background says it's her turn to talk about what her daddy does. The little girl grabs a piece of paper from the tabletop in front of her and holds it up. It's a photograph of a soldier in combat gear standing by an armored vehicle in a desert. The photograph is pasted onto a piece of paper with drawings of hearts, flags, and what I assume are eagles surrounding the photo.

"Oh," I realized. "I've seen this one. It's so sweet."

"You and six million others," Cal said.

The little girl starts talking in the pure tone of toddlerhood, the voice everyone seems to have at that age before life starts changing the key. She speaks of how far away he is, how he is keeping everyone safe. A figure appears behind her.

"Here it comes," I narrated, my tears welling up. "I'm going to lose the dare again."

The camera zooms out to reveal her father behind her. I was so absorbed in the moment that it took me a couple of seconds before I recognized him.

I didn't say, "Hey, it's you."

Instead I turned to look at him in person next to me.

He kept watching the video.

"Nobody ever recognizes me. I'm just a uniform. My little girl is the star of the show."

The camera dashes around behind him to catch her reaction as he taps her on the shoulder.

She turns and starts to cry at the sight of him, a joyful cry, with the kind of force that usually takes several seconds or even minutes to reach. But she reaches that force in a single moment. She stays in her seat and keeps crying and staring, as if she isn't sure that he's really there. She slowly climbs out of her chair and approaches him, never taking her eyes off him. He kneels down and she hugs him, and she somehow reaches an even higher level of emotion. She buries her head into his shoulder and the camera stays on them for a while. The person behind the camera eventually seems to realize it's time to leave them alone. The picture jerks around as the person forgets to turn off the camera as they lower it. They hold it back up and steady for a moment, apparently suspecting they were still recording. A voice says "oops," then the video ends.

Freeze frames of other recommended videos pop up on screen. All of them feature soldiers returning home.

Cal exited the program before the next one could play.

"Ours is the best," he said.

"I agree," I freed some tears from my eyes with the back of my hand.

"I especially don't like the ones filmed in front of a big crowd, like at a high school football game," he went on. "How many people do you need watching your private moment?"

"Six million?" I kidded.

He grinned.

"We did it before it was a thing."

"I like the ones with dogs," I said.

"Me too. Or dogs and kids."

"Those are the ultimate."

"Funny thing is," he said. "It's not the way I remember it."

"The video?"

"The moment. That day. I watch it as if I'm one of the six million. Like it's someone else."

"You don't remember anything?"

"I remember the feeling. But the actions..."

He shrugged.

"It was a lot to take in," I said.

"I wonder if that's how my whole life would seem if I could watch a video of it."

"Why did you leave them?"

I seemed to finally catch him by surprise with a question.

"Maybe they kicked me out."

"Your six-year old daughter kicked you out," I let him hear how ridiculous that sounded.

"My wife. You know what I mean."

"Did she?"

Cal slowed the pace.

"I'm not sure at this point," he genuinely tried to remember. "I left. But she didn't try to stop me."

"Why?"

He released a long sigh, and looked around at the television screens and computer monitors that surrounded us at eye level.

"Security," he said, the electronics appearing to remind him of the answer. "It's all I had to give."

I waited for him to continue.

"I saw some awful things. I saw what's possible. I know I've said I don't remember a lot. But that's when it comes to the order of things. I remember images. And I imagined those images with my family in them. I was so afraid, I forgot to love them. I mean, I did. I do. But the more I loved them, the more it would hurt to lose them. There were so many ways to lose them. So I decided the least I could do was protect them. I was good at that. But I realized having a gun by my bed wasn't enough. Someone could get the jump on us while I was sleeping. So I stood guard. I stayed up as long as I could, and slept during the day. I figured daytime was safe enough."

He looked as exhausted as he must have felt after one of those nights standing guard. I wouldn't have been surprised if he fell asleep standing up right there, in the middle of all the televisions and computers with something different showing on each one.

"We're not in a war zone, Cal."

I tried to be comforting. He tried to be appreciative.

"I know that, Fina."

"And nobody is coming after you, or your family."

"Things can change so fast."

There was more I could have said. But they were so standard, and he was so tired. I decided the best I could do was take him home and let him rest.

He nodded off a few times during the drive. When I dropped him off, I had a feeling that he may sleep for a couple days straight. As he shut the door of that big boxy house on the skinny lot that split the road from the railroad tracks, he may as well have pulled up a drawbridge from over a moat that flowed around his castle.

I regretted asking him those questions. I was afraid I may not see him again. I decided to leave him alone until our next sewing class. It was going to be a long wait. If he didn't show up to class, I would give myself permission to call. But I was sure he would be there. I was just as sure that he wouldn't call me before then.

I thought of the poetry he wrote. He wasn't completely against sharing. Not when what was on his mind could disguise itself. I wondered if he was thinking too much about his situation, or too little. The thousands of words I was using to make sense of what happened between us would probably be a short poem to him. Maybe he was right. Poems are all we add up to. Or maybe that was all he was capable of. I wondered how much control he had over his thoughts.

When I arrived home, I found the door to Zola's room shut. I didn't knock. Cal's story of defending his family was on my mind. I listened for a clue that she was in there. I heard the bed creak, or the floor. I wanted to protect her as much as Cal wanted to protect his daughter, but was it love, or did I feel obligated? I wanted to connect with Zola, but was it to help her, or claim victory in our battle of wills?

If I knew, I wouldn't have to write it all down.

I shied away from the door, taking long, slow, quiet steps.

CHAPTER IV

I knew exactly what I was doing when I settled on Mike. I told some of my closest friends. I told my mother. I told everyone I trusted that I was settling on Mike. I told him I was settling on him, without actually using the word "settle". I told him we made a great team. I told him how happy he made me as I gave him a peck on his lips before he could open them. When he wanted to wander off our firmly-trampled sexual path, I told him we weren't like that. We didn't need those things to prove our love.

I settled with pride.

Recovering from a passionate, bad relationship will do that to a person. That's the easy answer. But it says marriage is all or nothing, perfect or horrible. And it's all about sex.

My marriage came up during my recovery. I mentioned I was lucky to have Mike by my side instead of my ex, who didn't stay by my side when I was healthy. I could only imagine the different ways my ex would have found to avoid me while my mind was out of tune, when it seemed like all my brain could do was scribble pictures of things I wanted to forget.

I must have made Mike sound a little too nice. I must have sounded like I was talking about a pet, or a child, because my therapist gave me some really good reasons why I had nothing to be ashamed of. I didn't come up with any of them. She was the one who told me marriage is supposed to make life easier, not harder. She told me people don't get married to cure cancer or colonize planets, they get married for companionship. And as fun as sex can be, it's about affection, and that can be expressed all sorts of ways.

"But we do have sex," I remember saying.

"I didn't say you didn't," she answered. "But when people talk about settling, they're usually talking about not having a sex life with their partner, or not a very exciting one."

"Then you're partially right," I admitted. "We do it…"

I completed my thought with a facial expression, the kind you give a friend when they ask how much you liked the mediocre movie, or the okay restaurant.

Releasing our sex life out into the open was such a relief. I brought it up on a coffee date after class with Hannah and Laurie. Cal was out of town. He was attending a funeral for a friend he had served with.

"Shouldn't be such a thing as settling for sex," Laurie agreed when I told her and Hannah what my therapist told me.

"But that's what people do," I said. "They think of settling as not getting any help around the house or with the kids."

"That's just wrong," Hannah chipped in.

"And the sex probably isn't as great as they think it is," Laurie added. "They just don't know any better."

As the conversation grew legs, I regretted starting it. Mike would be mortified. I often didn't realize I was sharing too much until after the information left my mouth, when it was in front of me taking on a life of its own. I tried to steer the topic in another direction without changing it, which was hard, because it required me to be subtle, and I was better at being obvious.

"Mike gets up in the morning before I do," I blurted out, then slowed myself down. "He gets ready for work. I have the bed to myself, and it feels so good. I lie on my back and stretch out, like I'm trying to touch all four corners of the mattress at the same time with my hands and feet. Then I'll take his pillows and put them in just the right places so I can turn over into the perfect position, like I'm suspended in mid-air, halfway between falling onto my stomach or rolling onto my back. I feel weightless. I feel free. And I hear him in the bathroom getting ready. The toilet flushes, the shower runs, the sink turns on and off a bunch of times, he brushes his teeth, blows his nose, groans every now and then. I like that, too. It's comforting. The freedom, the routine. I like them both."

"You're lucky you have both," said Laurie.

I smiled.

"I am," I agreed. "I certainly am."

I wondered if Cal's friend from the service had committed suicide. I knew that was a problem for a lot of combat veterans, and I was concerned about him. I searched the web for recent obituaries of young men who had served, who were from Utah. Cal had been guarded about where exactly he was going, but he let it slip that he had "a long drive to Utah" ahead of him. I found a link that fit the key words. The soldier in the picture looked much younger than Cal. I imagined Cal being a mentor to him. There was no mention of an accident or an illness.

I had memorized the picture pretty well, but was having a hard time recalling some of the details when Hannah snapped me out of it.

"Fina?" she asked. "Are you okay?"

I smiled at her and said that I was, then took a sip of coffee.

It was cold, and woke me up even more.

"The best part is when he kisses me," I fell back on my thoughts of mornings with Mike. "I'm half awake, and he bends over to kiss me goodbye. Sometimes it's a stretch. He has to work for it, because I'm twisted like a pretzel in the middle of the bed. But he does it. And we tell each other to have a good day."

"Aw," cooed Hannah, sounding more like the teenager she was than she usually did. "I want that when I grow up."

Laurie smiled at me, and I had a feeling she was looking right through my diversion.

I stared at the table. I didn't want to look as though I was addressing her.

"If I wasn't with Mike," I said. "I would rather be alone."

"Usually something is better than nothing," Laurie said. "But loneliness is better than a bad relationship."

Hearing her voice was a relief.

I glanced up and she winked at me. There was an opportunity for her to talk about any personal experiences that may have led her to that conclusion, but she wasn't the type.

So the opening sat there. I filled it before it could grow too large and uncomfortable.

"Besides," I said. "Have you seen me lately?"

"Now stop that," Laurie warned me.

"What?" Hannah wondered aloud.

I ignored Laurie and answered Hannah.

"I wouldn't exactly be a hot commodity in the singles scene."

They showered me with assurances that I honestly was not fishing for. I only wanted to hide my feelings for Cal. But all of their compliments led me to think that maybe he could have feelings for me, too.

It didn't matter. Finding someone to settle with was as rare as finding true romance.

What else was there but divvying up errands? Sitting places together and talking about our to-do lists? And even when our conversations stumble into the great questions of life, what do we have to offer in response but clichés?

Reminding myself of what makes a good settler wasn't helping. Not like it used to. While Mike and I wondered what dish to bring to a potluck, Cal and I wondered what the future held for humankind.

We decided it was to entertain and to clean.

I thought it would be a good idea to spend more time with Mike. I asked to come to work with him and help out with the residents when they went on their field trips. I had done it before, every so often while I was still at the state hospital.

I stopped volunteering when my disability started.

It would be a valuable way to fill my time, Mike said.

And he was right.

I said Zola was at a fragile age, and I wanted to be there for her.

She was, but didn't want me creeping around her. That's how she put it.

The real reason I didn't spend more time at Mentor Manor had to do with the residents. They struggled with feeling useful, with being part of the world. I was feeling the same without my job.

"They feel a lot more useless than you do," Mike said. "You'll come out of there feeling great."

He may have been serious. I looked at him long enough to give him a chance to prove that he was joking.

Not that he didn't have a point. I thought the same thing, but I was also afraid being around them could have the opposite effect. I would start to sympathize with them too much, agree with them too often, and instead of trying to lift them up or feel grateful for my situation, I would complain along with them. I wasn't sure I had the bubbles to stay bubbly long enough. That's really why I refused.

So when I asked Mike if I could come with him, he figured I wanted to feel better about myself. He didn't suspect I wanted to feel better about him.

The bus was the type you'd see shuttling people between airports and hotels. Instead of a hotel logo, the back of our bus was decorated with a huge photo of an old man and an old woman smiling together, wearing Hawaiian shirts, as though Mentor Manor was a cruise ship line rather than a retirement home.

We did drive the residents to a lot of fun and interesting places, to zoos and museums and operas and ballgames. Most of the destinations were hours away, so they wouldn't talk much during the drive. Maybe for the first fifteen minutes, then they would preserve their energy by dozing off or staring out the window.

I would spend the drive following our path on the GPS that was mounted on the dash of the bus. Mike would detach it and let me hold it. I would zoom out to get a big picture of where we were, and where we would end up if we veered off on certain highway junctions. I would zoom in on country roads that seemed to go nowhere to see where they ended up. For all of the fretting Cal and I did over technology, I loved being able to know exactly where things were, and where I was in relation to them. Maybe we weren't really fretting over technology. It was just something to talk about.

"What's down this road here?" Mike pointed to an empty road ahead of us that ran away from the highway with no buildings in sight. "I've always wondered. It's got the word 'Hot Springs' in the name. Is there really a hot springs out there?"

"Don't know why they'd lie about that," I followed its trail on screen as the road itself stayed in our window for a few moments, and then disappeared behind us.

The line on the screen led to a lodging icon at the base of the mountains several miles in the distance. I clicked on it and the name of a place came up with two reviews, for an average of one star. There was a quote under the star. It said, "Disgusting and scary."

"There's a hot springs all right," I told him.

"Oh yeah?"

"Yeah..."

I looked it up online to give it more of a chance. I found some pictures. It was a dusty lot with a few mobile homes parked around a couple of tubs.

"Not very encouraging," I said.

"Good to know," he smiled. "And to think there was a time when we would have had to drive all the way out there to find out."

"It would be an adventure," I looked on the bright side of the days before the web.

I was hoping he would defend his point. I wanted him to say we never would have taken that adventure, that we know more about the mysterious hot springs by looking it up than we ever would have in the days before we could.

But he shrugged and said, "That's true."

I made my own argument.

"Then again," I said, "it could be the last adventure we'd ever go on. It looks like a great place to murder someone. Or two."

Mike chuckled and drove.

It wasn't fair to expect the same kind of conversation I had with Cal. Mike had strengths of his own. I could rely on him to agree with me and adore me.

I wondered if those were still strengths, or if they were fantasies of a younger woman that are better off not realized. I was being coached into believing marriage shouldn't be a challenge, which made perfect sense, but was starting to think it should also help you prepare for challenges and deal with them. Assuring you that you're right, no matter what, didn't seem like much help.

I would help the residents off the bus and escort them around the grounds, or to their seat. It wasn't hard work, except for the glimpse of the future they made me face.

They were driven by pain and caution. Even at the height of joy, they would catch themselves. Getting lost too deeply in a moment could result in an unconscious move that would inflict pain, so they remained cautious at all times to protect the time they had left.

I let my mind wander between innings of the baseball game, or as I stared at a bear in the zoo trapped behind a moat and a high fence. I watched the most dramatic moment of the opera and wondered how it would feel to be so cautious as an older person, knowing you were always so cautious when you were younger, and if taking more risks when you could made the fear of pain later on any easier. But too many risks could keep you from even getting there. I had already used up a lot of chances.

I sat in the empty bus with Mike. There were certain shopping centers we stopped at along each highway where the residents could use the restrooms. When it was just the two of us and a bunch of empty seats, I thought "What else is there?"

Then the residents would slowly start to come out from behind the doors of the stores that let them use their bathrooms. They would refill the seats, and the bus became a chamber of complaints, about their aches, their regrets, about how different the world was now, and I thought about how I should spend my time before I found myself in the back of such a bus.

I thought about Cal.

CHAPTER V

Bonding with her mother wasn't the only reason Hannah took sewing classes. She also wanted to make her own costumes for the anime conventions she like to attend. She was still buying her costumes, and they weren't cheap.

She modeled one for us. She was heading to a convention soon and we begged her to wear it to class. We surrounded her outside the studio and fawned over her while we waited for Joyce to emerge from the house.

She wore a light blue wig with pig tails as thick as horse tails that reached below her knees, a shiny black mini skirt with light blue trim that looked like a French maid outfit from outer space, and thigh-high black boots. She told us the Japanese name of the character, but we were more interested in what it did. We couldn't quite understand.

Hannah explained she was a vocaloid, a character who sings songs written for her.

"So it's a cartoon version of a singer," I tried to follow.

"An animated singer," Hannah sort of agreed. "Yes."

"And it has the same name as the singer."

"There is no real person. Just the vocaloid."

"But somebody has to sing the songs," Laurie said.

"Yes," Hannah was being very patient with us. "But we don't know their name."

"Singers are willing to do that?" Laurie couldn't believe it.

"Their voices go through a lot of software. It sounds different by the time it's produced. I'm not sure you even need to be a good singer to make it work."

"But it's still pretty much like lip-synching," I said.

Hannah hesitated.

"There's no person pretending to sing," she said. "On stage, there's a hologram. It's more like being a puppeteer."

Cal laughed.

"What?" Hannah sounded defensive for the first time.

"Nothing," Cal said. "I've always thought the word 'puppeteer' is funny."

Joyce finally appeared and walked past us, trying to get her smile right. She didn't seem to notice anything different about Hannah. She opened the studio and suggested we get to work.

"So can you teach Hannah to sew something like that?" I asked Joyce, in search of a reaction.

"I already am," she said, and left it at that.

We were still trying to figure out the vocaloid's place in the world after class at the coffee house. Hannah suggested we come with her to the convention. Laurie, Cal, and I looked at each other. A road trip with Cal sounded wonderful.

"What's your schedule that weekend?" I tried to make eye contact with both Laurie and Cal.

"I'm free," Cal shrugged.

"Me, too," Laurie agreed.

"You can crash in the hotel room with me and my friend," Hannah offered.

All three of us shot that down at once, without having to look at each other.

"We're too old," Laurie said, while Cal and I made disagreeable noises and shook our heads.

"We'll find a room of our own," I said.

"Maybe three," Laurie added.

"Might be hard to find one on a convention weekend," Hannah warned us.

She was right.

I agreed to be the point person and almost gave up. I finally happened upon a cancellation at a hotel not far from the convention center. Closer than Hannah's hotel, it turned out.

Even though Cal and I were going to share the room with Laurie, it was still our first road trip together. We drove together in his truck. Laurie had to work and couldn't take off until Friday evening, so Cal and I went Friday afternoon to check in.

It wasn't really necessary. We could have called and let the front desk know we wouldn't be arriving until around nine, but I wanted to feel what it was like to be on the road with Cal.

He went along with it. He didn't point out the flaws in my plan. I liked to think it was because he wanted to be alone with me, too, for a few hours. But Laurie went along with it as well. She could have suspected something and was letting us play it out, but she was so straightforward, not at all crafty. She would have teased us the moment the idea came to her. More than likely, they both simply thought that checking in earlier was a good idea.

"I can't decide if I'm being a gentleman or not," Cal said as we stood in the doorway of the hotel room and looked at the two beds. "I'm giving you and Laurie your space, but I end up with more room."

"We're fine."

"I could request a cot from housekeeping."

"Nonsense."

"I've slept in much worse."

"They're queen-size beds. Plenty of room."

I had yet to flirt with him in all the hours of our conversations.

I gave it a try.

"And if Laurie makes a move on me, you can watch."

"You think she'll mind?" he rolled with it.

"I'll tell her that's the only way it happens."

I would have liked to pick up on more sexual tension, but at least I didn't bomb. I got a laugh out of it.

We had agreed to meet Hannah for an early dinner at a buffet across the street from the convention center. We made good time on the road and arrived earlier than planned, even though we had mostly taken lesser-known highways that ran parallel to the interstate. Cal wanted as few cars around him as possible when he drove.

There was hardly a moment of silence the whole way.

When there was silence, it was a satisfying kind of quiet. It was a chance to consider the vastness of the sky and the land and our place in between them. There were so few clouds, and the horizon was one story high. The trees were in orchards. The water flowed through cement canals. The rest of the land was a dry reminder of what everything would look like if there were no people around.

We passed by a mileage sign with three upcoming places listed. The last one looked odd. Instead of a Spanish or Portuguese name, it sounded British. Something "Gardens" or "Park". The first name was along the lines of "Windsor" or "Kent". I was keeping an eye on our position on my phone, following the blue dot that represented us on the GPS map. I scrolled ahead and couldn't find any such town. I almost forgot about it, since it was the farthest place past the sign. But thirty miles later, I was scanning the countryside without really looking, trying instead to think of a point to make about something Cal said, and there it was.

There was an abandoned cluster of about ten houses with just enough of the conceited name still visible on a buckled wooden sign. Not even the most desperate farm worker could have lived in any of the homes. Every roof had been stripped of its shingles and appeared to have at least one huge, splintery hole. The frames were visible. Shredded pieces of the walls remained, every inch sprayed with graffiti.

I looked at my screen. Our blue dot was floating along a line with nothing around it. I zoomed in. There was a grid. A few streets off the highway where the broken homes huddled. But there was no name.

I forgot what I was trying to say and pointed out the ghost neighborhood to Cal. I wondered what the place was supposed to have been. A town? A housing development? A business district? He said he didn't know. All he knew was that it represented everything we own, and where it all ends up.

Then he apologized for being morbid.

I thought back to the first few sewing classes, when he hardly said a word. I considered the difference and smiled.

He caught me smiling and asked me what was up. I changed the subject by suggesting a game of "I Spy". We played for a dozen miles or so, and twice I had to say, "I spy someone driving too fast." I remember that because it meant he was enjoying himself enough to lose track of our speed. It was a good sign.

Not safe, but a good sign.

It left us with an hour until our dinner with Hannah, so we each stretched out on a bed and watched the Food Network.

Cal fell asleep.

I enjoyed waking him when it was time to go. I could have watched him sleep a lot longer, but didn't want him to wake up and find me hovering. I thought that would kill any chance we had.

On our way to the restaurant, we passed hundreds of people in costume, walking along as though it was just another day. They talked, checked their phones, held hands, but wore ninja veils and chainmail hoods and all kinds of fantastic hand-crafted weapons slung across their backs. I recognized the occasional Star Wars character, and a few from video games I had seen commercials for, but most were a mystery. They could have been real outfits, fashion trends, as far as I knew.

"Getting away from themselves for the weekend," Cal said as we walked past a huge teddy bear with a massive head that caused the person inside to wobble a bit.

"I don't know," I said as I veered away from the bear. "It seems like this is a big part of who they are."

A group of girls in matching beige military-looking uniforms carrying elaborate cardboard guns mingled on the sidewalk between us and the entrance to the restaurant. I worried that Cal may have a flashback. They looked enough like a small army to me.

But not enough to trigger anything in Cal.

Which made sense when I compared his condition with my own.

Sight usually had no knack for chasing my memories. It was touch, temperature, sounds. Like at the solar farm. What he could see of the repairman was blurred. Once the vision became clear, there was no room for imagination. The heat could let the mind wander, and the noises, all you can feel but not see. The girls in costume were clearly girls in costume. Maybe if we encountered them in a dusty town in the desert in the summer with gun shots in the distance. But they were in front of a convention center in a big city with mild temperatures and laughter in the background.

We politely fought our way through them and entered the buffet.

Hannah was waiting for us at a table in her vocaloid costume. She pointed out another young woman dressed as the same character on the other side of the restaurant.

"I got a table close to the door so you wouldn't see her first and get confused."

"We know our Hannah when we see her," I hugged her as she stood to greet us.

"Plus that one is sitting with Super Mario and a couple of bosses from Mortal Kombat," Cal said.

Hannah and I looked at him. We were impressed and surprised.

"I played a little in the service," he explained. "Lots of down time on the base."

"Where is your friend?" I asked as we made our way to the buffet line.

"She didn't want to eat this early. She's at a panel."

"You're so patient with us old people," I said.

"What's a panel?" asked Cal.

"People cosplay characters from a show and answer questions from the audience."

"Anyone from the actual shows ever come?"

"If they do, they come as themselves, as the actor. Not as the character."

"So actors are the only ones acting like themselves at these things."

Cal let that one hang there so we could admire it, or tease him about being a fuddy duddy. We did a little of both as we went our separate ways at the food stations and met again back at our table.

"I think I saw a few more vocaloids," Cal said.

"I know I did," Hannah confirmed.

"Why can't someone dressed like you guys do it?" he asked. "Why does it have to be animated and projected?"

"I thought we already covered this at Joy's house," Hannah sighed.

"I never weighed in," Cal said. "But I've been thinking about it."

"Thinking too much about it," Hannah corrected him.

"No, really," Cal persisted. "Why the hologram? With the digital voice? It's just an elaborate pantomime. People could do it. Maybe even better."

"People dig vocaloids, Cal," she said. "If they didn't, you wouldn't see so many of us around."

"People go to concerts dressed like their favorite singer," Cal said.

"Not really," Hannah slowly formed her words.

"Sure they do," Cal snapped back. "KISS...Madonna..."

"Yeah," Hannah caught up to his pace. "Singers who wear costumes, or go through phases."

"People dress like rappers, or band members," Cal said.

"That's fashion."

"Dress too much like them, it looks weird," I added. "Like you're stalking them."

I wasn't sure why I was taking Hannah's side. I must have grown used to debating Cal.

"But dressing up like someone, something that doesn't exist," Cal said. "That's normal?"

"Maybe not normal," Hannah said. "But safer. There's nothing to live up to. If I'm not as pretty as my favorite singer, or don't look like her, I'm not going to bother. But with cosplay, there's nothing to lose."

Cal smiled.

"I see your point," he said. "Thanks for putting up with us."

"Speak for yourself," I kidded.

"Thanks for putting up with me," he corrected himself.

We ate the food standards on our plates, and watched people.

An old man at a table across the aisle from us and a few booths down caught our eye. He clutched a mug of coffee and gazed around the room at the costumes. We wondered between us what he might be thinking.

We had forgotten about him and moved on to the next subject when he stood up and tapped on his mug with a butter knife, as though proposing a toast.

"Can I have your attention?" he announced.

His voice was not very loud. He strained to be heard. It was more the sight of him that grabbed people's attention. He was dressed as if serving as an example of how to dress with dignity in old age. He stood as straight as he could manage. Our section listened like children about to be read a story.

"You are clearly people of great imagination," he said. "Would you please do me the honor, then, of imagining something with me?"

More sections fell silent. He had most of the dining room either listening to him, or wondering what he was saying.

"My wife and I came here almost every day, around this time, since this establishment opened ten years ago. We usually sat right here, where I'm sitting today. She died nine months ago."

The silence was lightly cracked by a few people saying "Aw."

"And I kept coming here and sitting in the same place. It's what we did. It brings me comfort. But I get frustrated sometimes. Not sad. We had a wonderful life together. We had a small family. One child, no grandchildren. All of my siblings have passed. So have my wife's siblings. I've been surrounded by beautiful people. But there aren't many left. Which is the source of my frustration. I want more people to know how fantastic my wife was."

The "aws" disappeared. They were replaced by sniffles.

"Please do me a favor. Imagine a woman around my age, out of my league, sitting at this table. She's smiling at you, asking you questions about your outfits. Then she asks questions about you. She's fascinated by you. She was fascinated by people, and the worlds they inhabit. She was fascinated by the world we all inhabit. Her name was Tilly, and she deserves to be remembered by more than just me and the staff here. They'll tell you. She was the best."

One of the servers waved a dish towel in the air and yelled, "Amen!"

Another server yelled, "You tell 'em, Ernie!"

The rest of the staff started applauding, and we followed. Soon the whole restaurant was cheering.

Ernie sat down. A group of characters lined up to shake his hand and exchange a few words with him. The gigantic teddy bear we saw walking down the street gave him a hug. Or maybe it was another person dressed as a gigantic teddy bear.

The three of us weren't sure what to say. We let the moment live on without comment. Anything we could have said would not have done it justice. It would have been as useful as saying "Aw."

We focused on our plates, on our helpings, and resumed a normal flow of conversation when we were ready. Hannah offered to show us around the convention.

We walked the enormous lobby, rode escalators to the next level, which seemed even larger, often taking small steps to make our way through all the people, all the characters. It was like being in an airport with no airplanes surrounding it, a big carpeted station where all these people in costume happened to find each other and were so happy to have it work out that way, they decided to stay. We ducked into ballrooms and conference rooms, listened to panelists for a few minutes, watched videos for a few scenes. We took a few laps around the merchandise floor, nodding at the booths.

Hannah did most of the talking as she guided our way. I did most of the responding. Cal mostly took it all in. He was especially interested in the booths where artists were selling their drawings. He stopped to watch them work, telling us he would catch up, or rejoin us when we made our way back around.

Hannah's friend texted her and asked to meet up at an AMV contest. She told me that meant "Anime Music Video" contest. I told her to go ahead, that I'd fetch Cal and we'd see her later, maybe with Laurie if she was up for going out when she arrived.

I circled the booths and didn't see Cal at any of them.

I went out into the lobby and saw him sitting at the top of a flight of stairs that overlooked the crowd.

"Good idea," I said as I sat down next to him. "Cheyenne got lost at Disneyland when she was little, and climbed a tree. All you need to do is scream 'Mom' over and over and you'd look just like her."

He smiled.

"I have an idea," he said.

"Let's hear it."

"It's an alternate reality. Like one of those stories where Germany wins World War II."

"Oh. That kind of idea."

"I used to wonder if our enemy got PTSD. I mean, of course they did. But they were so damned determined, like they had nothing to lose. Real balls-out kind of stuff. So I wondered. And I read that they did. But then I wondered if it was different somehow. If their pain had a twist. I tried to put myself in their position, but that was impossible.

I had no idea what it would be like to live there. I would have to start from the beginning. I would have to be born and raised in a town I've only passed through fully armed. I would grow up playing games and having conversations I can never imagine, being taught things I've tried to understand but never really can."

He gestured out at the hive of costumes and gave me a knowing look.

"You know..." he joked.

"I know," I agreed.

Which is where the alternate reality came in. He said if he couldn't accurately go back to the beginning of a life on the other side of the world and think it through to the point where he took up arms, he could instead imagine growing up in a version of the United States that got off to a very different start.

I had a hard time following his story at first. I understood what he was getting at, and it all came together clearly at the end. But the early parts included some history that I needed to look up later on. He talked about the Articles of Confederation, the War of 1812, the kinds of things that are sometimes studied but never celebrated.

The United States never became united. The Constitutional Convention ended in an impasse. Each state was its own country. Every country had something valuable in it, but not everything it needed. They fought over roads and waterways. Wars would break out, and countries from Europe and Asia would take sides. The tiny countries were the world's playthings. When oil was discovered in the Middle East, it was pretty much left alone. Everyone wanted a piece of North America. Virginia would invade Ohio, and England would get involved for the lumber. Missouri would invade Texas, and Japan would get involved for the oil. And the entire western half of the country was under the control of warlords. The unified, wealthy powers of the world met to create boundaries. They drew lines and mapped out new countries like Utah and California, and gave control of each one to a different tribe, made them a royal family, in exchange for a cut of what they wanted from the land. Meanwhile, the United States of Arabia emerged. They used their great wealth to become the biggest superpower on earth. And they wanted to create a United States of America, a friendly source of revenue.

Cal imagined himself in such a world. He thought of his small hometown relying on aid from foreign countries, because the government was a family business that barely functioned outside of the capital city. People came from faraway places and told them what to do in a language they couldn't speak. He remembered the worst job he ever had in the real world, the feeling of helplessness that comes with needing the job but hating it, knowing you could do better if you had the chance, but not having the chance. He imagined that same feeling applied to his alternate world, the upside-down place where he was born and raised. The young men in pickup trucks with angry bumper stickers would actually have a good reason to be angry. The Christians claiming persecution because people say "Happy Holidays" during Christmas would actually be persecuted. The angry and the religious would join forces, each one needing the other to strengthen their cause.

There would be no send-offs at an airport or a train station to go off to war.

"I would just run down the street," Cal said. "Just follow the sounds of gunshots and explosions and screams. I would probably be a better soldier. Not better trained. But completely dedicated. The goal would be so clear. The good and bad so black and white. And when it was over, if I survived, I wouldn't be the only one who was ruined. It would be my neighborhood. My home. So yeah..."

He stared ahead of him, no longer at the crowd below. He stared through the air at something on the other side of the center, the giant window maybe, or the beams that held up the ceiling.

"PTSD might be very different, depending on where you're from," he said. "Depending on everything."

I reached out and held his hand.

We had hugged before, but this felt more intimate. Less of our bodies touched, but it lasted longer.

It lasted for an hour, wordlessly, as the sun set through the windows. I could feel our hands go through changes. Our grip would loosen and tighten, our skin moisten and dry. Sometimes I could feel blood flowing beneath the surface. Between our fingers a pulse, and I wasn't sure whose it was.

CHAPTER VI

A young woman came out of Joyce's house to let us into the studio.

We were surprised when she introduced herself as "Joy's daughter, Mindy."

"You're so friendly," each of us seemed to say at least once before Joyce came in to take over the class.

"So friendly…"

"Did you even know I existed?" Mindy grinned.

"To be fair," I said, "we never asked."

"And Mom comes across as so open to questions," Mindy's grin grew. "Such an open book."

"A book on what?" Laurie muttered.

Joyce entered.

She caught up with Mindy's smile, but couldn't catch the eyes.

"Thank you, dear," she said to her daughter.

"You want to hang out after class?" Mindy asked us.

"We always do," Laurie said. "Join us."

Mindy considered that great news.

"All right," she said. "See you then. Have a good class."

She directed it more toward us, with a glance at her mother on the way out.

Joyce passed out some spare pieces of cloth to each of us and told us to practice a lock stitch before working on our current projects.

I complimented her while we worked. I told her what a nice daughter she had.

"Thank you," she nodded.

A few minutes later, Laurie added how much she liked Mindy, too.

Joyce thanked her, too.

We all looked at one another on the sly. Hannah held out for another few minutes before offering her compliments.

Joyce thanked her as though it was the first one.

It was Cal's turn, but he shrugged at us.

"There's no rattling Joy," he said as we recalled our game at the coffee house.

That was true. But it was fun to try.

And Cal not trying much of anything fit a pattern since we had been back from the convention.

It was hard to say when Cal was being distant. It was more accurate to say he was sometimes more distant than usual.

Maybe it started after we stopped holding hands at the top of the stairs.

Laurie had appeared in the crowd below us. We saw her first.

I think.

She may have spotted us earlier, and was working her way toward us.

We swiped our hands away from each other.

She waved.

"Do you think she saw us?" I asked.

Cal shook his head. It could have meant he didn't know.

She said she didn't text me because she wanted to wander around and take it all in and happen to run into us.

Cal and I didn't look at each other much for a while. I thought it was because we were looking for signs from Laurie. When the coast seemed clear, he smiled at me. He smiled a lot.

Only days later, over coffee, did I think maybe he was smiling as if to say, "How could I have done that?"

At the time, it was so encouraging and scary. It felt like the beginning of something sure to be a memory. Hannah and her friend joined us for a while, but not for long. Laurie was more leery of the convention than we were. She added a skeptical presence that wasn't there when the girls had first spent time with us. They loved what they were doing, knew it may be considered weird, and weren't in the mood to defend it. We were on their turf, after all.

I was loving what we were doing, too. What Cal and I were doing. And when it came to Laurie, she either didn't notice, or had no problem with us.

Maybe there was nothing there. Maybe that's why she didn't notice.

Even the doubts I had at the coffee house made me feel young again. I enjoyed them for that reason. Everything had been so certain for so long. Mike would be there for me. I would be there for everyone. Even the uncertainties were set. Zola would resist me. Cheyenne would ignore me. I relished the chance to be breathless about something.

"She's like God," Mindy said about her mother. "She created my world, then left it at that."

"A God you can see," Hannah said.

"Well..." Mindy hemmed.

"And it's not a God you necessarily want to smile on you," Laurie added.

"That smile," Mindy groaned. "It somehow got worse over the years."

"As long as she runs a good sewing class," I said, suddenly very protective of Joy.

"I'm not looking for her approval," Cal agreed, without looking my way.

"Well," he corrected himself. "Except when it comes to my sewing."

"Psst," Mindy lowered her voice. "That approval is never coming."

Then she laughed as though she had been drinking margaritas instead of coffee.

"I don't really care," Cal explained himself again. "It was a joke."

"You need to work on your delivery," Mindy said.

"I wouldn't disagree with that," Cal said. "I can be hard to read."

I wondered if that was directed at me.

I wasn't normally so self-centered. At least I tried not to be. But I had reason to believe it was for me.

We had walked side-by-side from the convention center back to the hotel. Laurie was next to us. Someone walking past would probably think we were keeping Cal between us as protection. Laurie was no more a third wheel than I was.

But Cal and I would brush forearms or fingers every several steps. I started to brew a fantasy of getting up to use the bathroom later that night. Laurie would be sound asleep. I think Cal is, too. But when I open the door to go back to bed, he's waiting for me. He doesn't startle me. I was hoping for this. I'm glad it's dark so I don't have to worry about what my body looks like. I can just feel. The only problem is noise. We start breathing heavily as we kiss.

That's what kept me from making it real later on, if that was even possible. I didn't want to wake Laurie. I didn't follow Cal when he got up to use the bathroom, and I hoped he wasn't there when I opened the door after I used it.

I was relieved, and slept well the rest of the night. I thought of sending him some flirty text to take the temperature of his reaction. But I was starting to enjoy the wondering. If there was no chance, I wouldn't know for a while longer. I could keep dreaming.

Mindy eased up on her mother eventually. We stopped asking questions. She didn't seem to know any more about her than we did. However hard Cal was to read, he was no Joyce.

"Let's take a moment to toast her, rather than roast her," I said in so many words, that didn't really rhyme. "If it wasn't for Joy, we would not have met. We wouldn't be here."

Everyone raised their cups and made cheery noises. We didn't bother clinking our cups, since paper doesn't clink.

Hannah mentioned Cal's rom com recovery program to Mindy, and we mostly talked about movies the rest of the evening.

Cal was having a hard time making eye contact with me. He didn't totally avoid it, but it would seem to happen by accident, as though he forgot I was there, and his eyes stumbled upon me. Then he would twitch into a brief grin, and his eyes would dart elsewhere.

For the first time I could remember, I wanted to make him feel bad. I thought of mean things to say. I chose a couple that I could throw at him in the parking lot instead of our long, pleasantly awkward good-nights.

There was still some sunlight left on the parking lot. I waited until the others had driven away before following him to his truck.

"Dammit!" he burst as he reached his door.

"This will only hurt a little bit," I joked.

I figured he knew I was going to call him out on dodging me.

"What?" he glared at me.

"Never mind."

"I locked my keys in the truck."

"Call the auto club."

"I don't want to waste a visit on something this stupid."

"That's a category they keep track of?"

"I have a spare at the house," he said, looking at me with hesitation.

"I'll give you a lift."

I sounded annoyed, but for a different reason than he probably thought.

The only thing he offered as we drove to his house was an excuse for why he left his keys in the truck.

"I have a lot on my mind."

He wouldn't say what.

So I asked.

"Everything."

I sighed and remembered my impulse to hurt him.

"You don't seem that bad," I said.

"What do you mean?"

"I get what you told me about defending your family. That's sad and all. But is it really so bad that you have to stay away from them?"

"What's this about, Fina?"

"You, Cal," I said. "As always. Everything is about you."

The next mile was quiet.

I was the one who was able to avoid eye contact. I enjoyed the power shift. Plus it was safer. I kept my eyes on the road all the way to his house.

"Don't look," he said as he opened the car door the moment we pulled into his driveway.

I had no idea what he meant. He seemed to think he was being funny.

He jumped out and fetched his house key from under the doormat and held it up.

"I told you not to look," his voice fought through my window.

I gave him a courtesy smile.

He unlocked the door, then barged into the house and ran out seconds later. He was breathless as he slid back into the car.

"Let's go, let's go!" he panted as though he was on a mission, being chased.

I thought about how people who aren't usually charming get so much credit for their little bursts of charm.

Thinking of that made it easy to keep my cool, which was more cold than cool.

I could feel his realization. He was like a fly starting to figure out it's not air, but glass he's trying to buzz through. If a fly knew what air and glass were.

This was new territory for me. Even at my lowest point, after my job was taken away in a dark room by a patient I had spent years helping, I was never rude to those who did anything short of spitting in my face. I wondered how long I could hold out.

I tested myself. I took a lot of side streets to reach the coffee house, waiting as long as possible to get on the busy road that skimmed past the shopping center.

On one of the dim streets, we passed a house perched on a slope. The slope held up a heavy collection of this and that, of the jettisoned and discarded, as though the house had tipped forward and its contents had spilled out onto the dry lawn. A car was parked in the driveway that had cobwebs hanging from the axles.

A man danced on the front porch. But he wasn't dancing. He was talking to himself so deeply that his body was swept up in whatever he was trying to convince himself of. I recognized him from some of the business districts. People often called the police when he managed to notice other people were around, and he thought they needed to hear what he had to say.

I wondered if the police brought him here instead of jail. I assumed there were family members inside the house who did what they could to keep an eye on him, but their eyes were tired.

I heard Cal softly laugh for one syllable as we passed the house.

"No," I heard myself bark.

"What?" he asked.

"You don't get this one," I said. "You don't get to use the broken man metaphor."

"Fina…"

"Admit it. You were going to mold that poor guy into a speech about where you would be if not for the grace of God or whatever. Don't. Just don't. No."

"I wasn't going to do that."

"Okay," I said, not sure if I believed him. "Then I will."

He laughed.

I pulled over and stopped the car.

"Shut up," I told him.

He did.

"I was as close as you ever were to being like that poor bastard. Maybe even more."

"I don't doubt it."

"What's that supposed to mean?"

"Oh, good lord…"

"You're right," I caught myself. "Sorry."

I exhaled and tried to calm myself down. I remember hoping Cal would reach over and at least pat my shoulder.

"I know you like to talk about it," he said, keeping his hands to himself. "I wish I could."

I started to laugh.

"What?" he asked.

"You still don't get it," I said as my laugh played itself out.

"Oh, but I do," he insisted. "I know it's not all about me. But I'm not going to ask you to share, because then I'll feel obligated. You show me yours, I show you mine. That's how it goes. And I'm done with all that."

We sat for a very long matter of seconds. The street was as quiet as we were. The sky was purple.

"It's the clichés," Cal said.

I remember the line clearly. It was short and simple enough.

But I wasn't sure what he meant.

I didn't tell him so, but my silence must have said something.

"The stories are unique enough," he explained. "Well, the details are. The plots are all the same. But people fill in the blanks with new names and places and action. That makes things interesting."

He sighed before continuing.

"Then we reflect. The storyteller comes to a conclusion, or the listener gives some advice. And there's no way to dress it up. We choose from the same old options, and the choice sounds very familiar."

"You just need to take it one day at a time," I played along. "Each day is a new beginning."

Cal laughed and pitched in one of his own. I think it was, "You can't learn to swim without getting in the water."

We kept looking straight ahead, through the windshield, while we talked.

"Mike used to find them on the web and print them for me," I said. "I'd find one in my dresser drawer, or tucked under the windshield wiper."

"At least you could throw those away," he said. "My wife bought light switch covers and calendars and framed posters. Complete with soothing pictures. Everywhere I turned there was a lighthouse aimed at me."

"Or a cloud with sunrays shooting out of it."

"So scripture, then?"

"He went with scripture sometimes. But other prophets weren't out of the question."

"Khalil Gibran?"

"Yup."

"Basho?"

"Pretty sure."

I waited for him to volley back.

The pause lingered.

I turned away from the windshield and looked at him. He was smiling at me.

"They're not wrong," he said.

"The quotes?"

"They may be tiresome, but they're right."

"Like a parent."

"Wouldn't know."

"Stop it," I told him. "You'll be fine."

"Once I show up."

"She won't remember this part. It'll be a story. And it may not even be told. If you don't piss anyone off."

"It could come in handy for someone, couldn't it?"

"Wife, mother-in-law."

We turned back again to look in front of us.

"There are parenting clichés that have been lost to us," I said.

"Like what?"

"Like 'this is just a phase' and 'it's such a small moment in your life.'"

"Why wouldn't I say that?" he said. "I like those."

"Because you know better. Your life, my life, they were changed in a matter of seconds. Very small moments."

"A higher degree of difficulty," he grumbled. "Just what I need when it comes to parenting."

"You'll be more honest."

"That's what kids want. A parent who's really open with them."

"Are you being sarcastic?"

"A parent who tells them everything."

"That's not what I mean," I said.

"What do you mean?"

"You won't sound like every other parent."

We said more before I started the car and drove him back to the parking lot, but it's not clear what. As soon as I told him he wouldn't sound typical, I got selfish again and thought of myself rather than his daughter. I imagined a future where the memory of him had faded, where I couldn't place his voice when I tried. That was the future awaiting me when he got back together with his family.

When he climbed out of my car, he placed his hand on the passenger window to shut the door. He left fingerprints that caught the light from the streetlamps in the parking lot.

I watched the prints fade from view as a blurry version of his truck drove away in the background of the picture framed by my window.

CHAPTER VII

I looked at his footprints in the dirt next to his truck.

He was there before me, inside our favorite lunch spot out in the countryside, holding a table for us.

He had started to show a lot more interest in spending time together right around the time I started to feel expendable.

I walked past his imprint, leaving my own alongside. The dirt was very thin, little more than layers of dust. The evidence of us would be gone by the end of the lunch rush.

I had been convincing myself that what I really wanted to do was help him. I wasn't falling in love, my story went. I was already in love with him in sort of the same way I loved my family. It was a love based on protection, on maternal instincts. That was how I could make a more permanent mark. I tried to think of him as I would my stepdaughter.

They had the most similarities of all the people I cared for.

The comparisons were pretty eerie when I lined them up. Or, maybe more honestly, when I lined up the ones that matched, and ignored the ones that didn't.

They both wrote angry poetry, both liked to stay in their room, and had to make an effort to be social. When they did, they were impressive.

Something I often failed to give Zola credit for is how fun she was to talk to when she was willing to talk and not simply talk back. Every so often, when the conversation interested her, she would seem to mature twenty years in the turn of a sentence. Suddenly the sullen tween appeared to be a character from one of those body-switching movies, where an adult and a child magically trade places. I don't know who the adult would be who lent themselves to Zola's body. Certainly not me or Mike. Some far-off person, a university professor or doctor of psychology.

Maybe Cal.

Hearing such words coming from Zola's pastel hair and furious wardrobe was no less shocking than hearing a voice in a burning bush.

I guess this is where her quirky interests came into play. I thought of what I was into at her age, what my daughter Cheyenne was into, the conventional pastimes like dance and sports. I was brought up to see those things as character building. And maybe they were. But they served up a pretty neat and tidy world view. We had mottos and slogans. Or to borrow from the conversation I had with Cal, we had clichés.

They were repeated by our coaches over and over, and ironed onto our shirts, as if we needed them in writing. A shirt was plenty of space to get their point across, again and again. Their point about going the extra mile, about going all out, about team work making the dream work. Whatever we were going with that year. They ended up being shifty foundations for adulthood. Not that they weren't true. In and of themselves, their advice is worthwhile. But circumstances matter. Turns out it's a lot easier to get pumped about things you're already into. Fortune cookie sayings about work and dedication become harder to apply to school work, and work in general. As aggravating as it was to see Zola look at everything with a sideways glance, her lack of illusions may have been paving an easier road into that real world. The world we never stop preparing for, and never quite seem to reach.

If only she wouldn't take it so far, so often. The ways she reminded me of Cal came to a screeching halt after a few connections between the lists. The biggest contrast was of course their reasons for writing their poetry and staying in their spaces. Zola's motivation seemed so unwarranted compared to Cal's. Her mother's disappearance was the closest she could come to the black hole that Cal swirled around. But even her attitude toward the mother caper flirted with the nonchalance she threw at everything else.

"Why wasn't there more of a search for her?" I asked more than once, and received the same answer in so many words.

"There wasn't that much publicity," Zola would say. "She was an adult. People aren't that interested in grown-up missing persons."

"But there was a child involved," was my reply. "You could make a plea, tug at people's hearts."

"It would be a waste of time."

"Why?"

"She wasn't pretty enough. Even a kid has to be cute. The older you get, the prettier you need to be. At her age, she needed to be raging-boner hot for people to care. She was all right, but not enough for a manhunt."

I wondered how her weary outlook would affect her search for love, if she bothered looking. She would likely never be in a bad relationship. There was that.

I never brought it up with her. She was a bit young. As if she would ever be interested in talking to me about love.

Just as well.

Loving Cal, and by loving I meant, at that point, loving him like a stepdaughter, was revealing to me what a worthless source of wisdom I was.

"I love this place," Cal said as he stared out the window at the empty route that passed by our country café.

"I love it too."

I thought about how we use the word 'love' too easily in the English language, how we need other words for different kinds of love. Like love of a place, or a friend, or a stepdaughter, or a friend who reminds you of your stepdaughter.

"That's one of my favorite things about where we live," he continued staring out the window. "These restaurants in the middle of nowhere that are really only ten minutes outside of town."

"It's nice to get away without having to go away."

He turned his attention from the window to me.

"It's probably chemical," he said.

I didn't get it.

"With Zola," he explained.

I had shared my thoughts about her before we had taken our window break.

"You mean puberty?" I asked. "That kind of chemical?"

"Unless you think it's the hair dye."

"Or the eye liner."

I considered the role of her changing body, which was easy to forget, buried under all of those costumes and props.

"I suppose it doesn't help," I decided. "But she wasn't exactly a Disney Princess before she hit her tweens."

I told him about the first time I met her, when she colored the children's menu black, and the last time I asked for her opinion on an outfit I had bought. She lowered her phone from in front of her face to size me up and down for a moment before going back to what she was doing without so much as a shrug.

"I would have preferred she laughed in my face," I recalled. "That she told me I looked like a maroon blimp, or whatever the color was. Maybe it was yellow. I mean, it was pretty butt ugly now that I think about it."

"That's the shame talking," he said. "I'm sure it was lovely."

"No," I chuckled. "It was bad. But to be dismissed like that. Like food that your cat sniffs and walks away from."

"That's why I don't own a cat."

"You should," I told him. "They're a perfect pet for males. I don't know why they didn't catch on more than dogs. Low maintenance, not the least bit needy, they can practically take care of themselves."

"The neediness is the whole point," Cal tried to keep his voice down. "The neediness without the conversation. You really don't know a thing about men, Fina."

"I don't know a thing about anything."

"You still know more than I do."

"Not true."

"Totally true."

"I know way less than you do."

"Wrong. I'm at a total loss when it comes to pretty much everything."

"You know why men like dogs."

"But I'm probably wrong, because I usually am."

"Usually?" I scoffed. "I'm always wrong. Every single time."

"There are tree stumps with a greater understanding of the world than me."

"Ask me a question. I won't have any idea what the answer is."

"What's two plus two?"

"Something that matters. Something important."

"Mathematics isn't important?"

"You know what I mean."

"No, I don't. Because I am utterly clueless about everything. Like I said."

Which may not have been the exact way the conversation went. But it was the exact moment when I stopped pretending I wasn't in love with him in the way people love each other who feel as though they've solved some great mystery by being together.

"I only stumbled onto that point about Zola because I can relate to her," he said.

I would have appreciated him making that connection a few minutes earlier. But now I didn't want to hear it. I tried not to laugh or scream over all the squiggly lines love traveled in. He took my silence as confusion.

"The chemical changes," he went on. "I feel physically different because of what happened. Like I've gone through a kind of puberty.

Maybe not in the way I look, aside from putting on weight. But changed physically as much as anyone who came back missing a limb."

I held my breath. Hearing him talk about his past felt like he was trying to say he loved me. I didn't want to say something wrong and scare him away from his reflection. I kept quiet and nodded ever so slightly, using the rhythm to keep a sincere look on my face.

"My life feels like a hallucination," he said. "I used to roll my eyes when I'd hear someone trip out over ideas like, 'Whoa, this is all a flashback happening just before the final moment, man,' or, like, 'Wow, maybe we're already dead and imagining life.' Now I fully relate. I feel like I may have died in battle, or I'm about to, and this is all a way to cope. At this moment I'm in shock and bleeding out on the other side of the world, and this scene here with you is made of morphine, the natural kind the brain makes to protect us when the intensity level breaks our meter."

Maybe I should have been hurt to hear there was a chance he thought I didn't exist. But even if I didn't, it felt good to know I was a figment of his imagination that offered comfort. I was tempted to say that maybe he was already in heaven, and I was an angel. That sounded like a pick-up line, though. A bad one. Unless he said it. Then it would sound great.

He didn't say it, of course.

It seemed to be my turn to say something. He was looking at me for a response, for approval.

"I think we're real," I said.

He laughed. I panicked.

"I didn't think what you said was weird at all," I assured him. "I have a good reason for believing we're really here."

"What's that?" he settled down with a grin.

"I'm so tired," I said. "A hallucination wouldn't be this tired. I feel like I've been at an amusement park all day, in the sun, and now I'm home."

"And all you want to do is sit on the couch," he agreed.

"Life is a gigantic couch," I played along.

"That sounds comfortable."

"But then your back hurts."

"And the crumbs start building up all over it."

"And you start to feel useless."

Cal smiled. It was a different smile than the one from a minute before. This new smile was relaxed. It was still a reaction to something I said, but less of a reflex. It built slowly, came from someplace deeper, as though it was self-made, arriving on its own terms.

"Sorry for doubting your existence," he said.

"It's pretty flattering," I said. "Everyone else thinks I'm all too real."

He leaned back into his smile and looked above me.

"What I wouldn't give for some boredom," he said.

"I can lend you all you need."

"That's a gift I wouldn't take for granted," he lowered his sights onto me again.

"You'd know how to handle it."

"It's the key to life," he said. "There's so much of it."

"Alone."

"That's right," he pounced on my point. "Loneliness and boredom, Fina. Face it."

"You're a fun date."

"Maybe I'm the hallucination," he said. "I'm the fears you must face."

I smiled.

He had a point about fear when it came to my relationship with him. But he didn't flinch when I used the word "date".

I thought about how much of our time we forget once it passes. When we reach the end, how much time we can truly recall, if we could put it all on a video. An hour? Two? Less than an hour? So many moments are gone forever as soon as they happen.

This was not one of those moments.

CHAPTER VIII

Cal stood in what looked like a huge fireplace. The walls were rippled black with burns. Dunes of ash were spread around a clearing in the center of the floor, where a pile of charred cabinets looked like firewood about to be lit, but also gave the strongest hint that the room had once been a kitchen. The appliances had all been pulled out. He stood in one of the empty spaces holding a crow bar.

"Perfect timing," he said. "I just finished ripping out the last cabinet."

"Do you help rebuild it, too?"

"Nope," he shook his head. "I'm the demolition crew."

"A one-man demolition crew."

He raised his crow bar and bellowed at the blasted ceiling. He quieted down and said "Let's rip up some pillows," before tossing the metal bar to the floor. It bounced and the sound echoed in my ears as we walked outside to his truck.

The truck bed contained the pillows he had worked on in class, with his poetry stitched into them.

"Weren't you afraid the pillows would fly out?" I asked.

"Maybe if I took the freeway."

"I've got mine in the trunk. Let's put yours in with mine when we're done."

We had agreed to give all of our pillows to Laurie. She wanted to start handing out gifts to clients, and was disappointed in her output. We were meeting her and Hannah for lunch, and the three of us were going to surprise her with our pillows.

First we needed to unstitch the darkness from Cal's.

He had taken to writing the poems on patches that he then sewed onto the pillows. Stitching the words themselves proved to be way too labor intensive. So most of the poems were easy to pluck. We saved the first couple he had made, with each word stitched in, for last.

"Unstitching them is an even bigger pain in the ass than stitching them," he said as we picked at the threads. "Isn't the old expression that tearing something down is easier than building it?"

"You have a knack for finding the exception," I said.

"The good news is, I can't see a robot doing this."

"Always looking on the bright side, too."

He looked at me as though he should also be flipping me the bird.

We sat in the vacant house, in the living room. It was strictly a kitchen fire. The rest of the house was lovely.

"The people couldn't stay here?" I asked.

"They could. My buddy told me they didn't want to."

"Why?"

"Too traumatic for them."

I stared at him as though he represented the family who had abandoned the house.

He noticed my expression.

"I'd say leave them your therapist's number on the fridge," he said. "But there is no fridge."

"I shouldn't judge," I caught myself.

"Probably lost some children's artwork," he encouraged me to keep judging.

"And maybe some stains that held some memories."

"Like that time they made spaghetti."

"Or that time they made a milkshake and forgot to put the cap on the blender."

"Stains are good souvenirs."

"Rings and necklaces are so fake."

"They're whatever you want them to be. Stains are the real deal."

Cal pulled the last thread from the pillow he was renovating and held it up for me to inspect.

"Any traces?" he asked.

"You can tell something was there," I studied the surface. "It's lighter where the words were. But you can't tell what they said."

"I want to test my memory," he handed me the pillow. "See if what I'm saying looks like it matches the evidence."

He recited a short poem, with a pause after every couple of words.

My nightmare

Says more

Each time

It calls

"I can definitely see some of the letters in the word 'nightmare,'" I said. "But the smaller words are just blobs."

We met Hannah on the way and combined all our pillows in my trunk. We beckoned Laurie over in the parking lot for the big reveal before we went inside for lunch.

She was so surprised and delighted that she didn't notice the scars left by Cal's poetry.

"These are your poem pillows?" she practically shouted when he asked if she could tell.

"Yup."

She grabbed one from the trunk and smacked him with it.

"You idiot!" she raised her voice even louder. "Are you sure about this?"

"Positive," he nodded. "They were undermining my rom-com therapy and lady lunches."

Laurie hugged him.

Cal was as surprised as we were. He managed to hug her back once it sunk in that this was happening, that she was really hugging him, and not pretending to wrestle him.

It was the last time the four of us would all be together.

We didn't know that.

We got our messages from Joyce after lunch.

I'm tempted to change the order of events. When I think about that afternoon, it feels like we knew. Eventually that will become the version we all tell. Class was cancelled, Joyce said she had to move because of her husband's job, so the four of us met for one last lunch.

Changing the order will change what we remember about our conversations. Knowing we would never meet again will bring more meaning to what was said, so what was said will have to sound more meaningful. We'll make sure it does.

I can still recall enough of the reality to remember it was a great afternoon on its own. It didn't need any help. It wasn't any more profound than any other time spent with friends, which is to say very profound. I don't know why we never met again as a group. I saw Hannah and Laurie individually, and of course Cal, but our four schedules never worked out for all of us to meet. We should have. We should meet every year until there's only one of us left.

We spoke about nothing that springs to mind. But I remember looking around the table at one point, I believe Hannah was talking, perhaps trying to explain to us why anime was different than cartoons, and I felt so wonderful about being there with them. I watched their expressions. Hannah looked so passionate, which is why I assume she was defending something that we dismissed as part of her youth. Laurie looked unconvinced, which didn't necessarily have to do with what was being discussed. It's just her. And Cal looked like he was trying to record everything, as though trying to push back against the idea that our brains are not stenographers.

I'd like to think I was smiling as I scanned their faces. I probably wasn't, though, because then someone would have asked why I was smiling, which would have disrupted the very thing I was smiling about. But I smile when I think about that meal now.

"It's all about feelings," Cal said outside after we had paid the bill and said our goodbyes to Hannah and Laurie.

We were at a restaurant in town, in a strip mall.

The wobbly man from the beaten house had wandered over from his world on the front porch and was taking a brisk lap around the center, passing the storefronts as though playing duck-duck-goose. I imagined the owners of each store hoping he didn't choose them. He passed where we had eaten and nodded at us in a way that would have looked completely normal coming from someone cleaned and dressed for work. He also said something that would have sounded completely bizarre coming from that same standard someone, but sounded normal coming from him. Something about dinosaurs.

We still had not heard from Joyce. That didn't happen until we had said goodbye and I was in my car. But Cal started to talk like we were never going to see each other again, which surprised me. It was as though we had already gotten the message.

"I know you don't like me using that guy to make a point," he said as we watched the man quiver away. "But honestly, I have no trouble imagining myself drifting around with him."

"I was upset that night," I said, letting him know it was okay.

"Or maybe we'd be rivals. Dueling lunatics."

"You could have an ongoing debate."

"And I'd never lose, because nobody would know what I'm talking about."

"Then he would never lose, either."

"That's a good way to stay friends," Cal realized. "If you're even aware of each other."

"You could have a dance-off."

"He would smoke me in a dance-off."

"You can do it," I offered mock motivation. "I can help."

"Aren't you glad you let me talk about him?"

"Assuming there's more to it than having some fun at his expense."

A few people came out of the restaurant and passed us on their way to the parking lot. We paused our conversation but held our ground. Cal picked it back up when they were out of earshot.

"The only reason I'm not debating dinosaurs with him and having dance-offs is because of the life I had before I left. The life that was still there for me when I came back."

"Are you saying that our broken man over there doesn't have a good family?"

"It doesn't matter. Maybe his family tried everything they could. Maybe they're awful. But his condition runs deeper than mine. He didn't need a war."

Cal looked over to check the man's progress. He was making the turn at the end of our walkway, a sharp left into the next bank of businesses.

"I don't have the right to compare myself to him," he said.

"It's not a contest."

He turned his attention back to me, kind of.

"The farther back you go, the less history talks about what happens to soldiers after a war. Battle X happened. It led to Y. And all the letters from the front sound heroic. All the memoirs of the survivors so noble. But those are the literate ones. They knew they were writing for history, for their place in it. Like if their words were good enough, they'd make it into the books. For every war, a writing contest. But then I think maybe they really didn't suffer as much, way back whenever. Maybe there was no PTSD, because life pretty much sucked all the time. Maybe war was an exciting distraction. It beat shoveling shit and fighting off the plague. I don't know. It's kind of like the story I riffed on at Hannah's convention, about whether the enemy ends up psychotic. I don't want to be alone."

"That's what the group therapy is for."

"I mean all of us. My generation. I want our history to be the same as the soldiers before us. I have this fear of being a weak link."

"You have plenty of company," I rubbed his arm.

"I owe my sanity to my family, but there's not enough of it for me to stay with them."

"You'll get enough of it back to get them back."

I wish that's what I said.

That's the line that makes sense now, when I think of the two of us in front of the restaurant with the bobbing figure of the broken man flickering in the corners of our eyes. It makes sense because the message from Joyce was about to arrive, which made me more confident about making my move, or maybe more desperate.

And making my move, I thought, would drive him back to his family, no matter how he responded. Whether or not we ended up spending time together as lovers, it was time that was doomed. I knew that going in.

CHAPTER IX

I gathered my supplies from my cubby hole. I was the last one to stop by the studio, so there was nothing left once my belongings were gone. All the spaces with our names on them were empty. I thought it might be fun to stay in the studio for as long as it took for Joyce to come in. I'd jump out and say "Boo!" Then maybe confront her.

But she was good at confrontation. She was good at it by avoiding it. She had that way of making it seem as though the question should not have been asked, the situation should not have reached such a point.

I probably didn't think about waiting for her. It seems like a good idea when looking back. Something I should have done, or thought of doing. I rarely think of doing the right or clever thing. With Cal waiting for me outside the gate, and me planning on making a move, I'm certain that's all I was thinking about. But it's my story and I want to look good in it. I don't want to come across as some bored housewife, even if I do have a dramatic backstory. The story itself, the one in the front, needs to be flattering. I want to have been thinking of amusing things.

I most certainly was not at that time, though. The memory fog is most thick when I recall the most important points. The fog rolls in on heightened emotions.

I remember being nervous. That's clear. I remember driving from Joyce's house to the front gate and thinking all the people who happened to be in their front yards or driveways were staring at me. And they were. But they always stared when we came and went through their neighborhood. It's what people in gated communities do. But I imagined they were judging me. They somehow knew I was a married woman driving out to hit on a married man. If I dared. I'm sure I remember more of them than there actually were. Two or three staring homeowners has grown to nine or ten.

Cal was still slumped behind the wheel. I didn't pull over. I gestured for him to follow me as I drove past. The coffee house was always the next step after Joyce's house. We had been plenty of other places together, of course, but none of them after class.

It was earlier in the day than class had been, earlier than we would normally go for coffee. But what I wanted to do needed to start with some normalcy. I needed to touch the routine before I broke it, as though sizing it up.

I suspect I laughed too hard at some of his lines, and talked a bit faster than normal. I prefer to believe our coffee conversation was fairly standard. Given what was underneath it, however, we most likely looked like we were on a first date.

Cal must have suspected something was different. He didn't seem surprised when I crossed the line. If I even crossed it.

We walked to our vehicles, which were parked next to each other.

All I said was, "I don't want to lose touch."

I don't think I said it suggestively.

When he kissed me, I realized I was crying.

"I'm sorry," I said as I pulled away.

"It's fine," he assured me.

"They're tears of joy," I assured him.

"Doesn't matter," he assured me. "Joy or sadness, I'm grateful for both."

We must have spent an hour leaning against my car, then his truck, making out like a couple of teenagers. My lips were about the only part of me that still felt young. The adrenalin rush pouring through my body reminded me how different it was the last time I was so out of my mind with lust for someone who was in front of me, touching me. The chemicals seemed to trace my figure, make a dopamine chalk drawing that contrasted the body I was sharing with Cal to the body I lived in when I couldn't get enough of Cheyenne's father twenty years earlier. And I didn't care, at least not yet. I wanted so much of him, so badly, that I feasted on his lips and the feel of him without a hint of self-consciousness.

The world had collapsed so fully into the two of us that we didn't notice the clouds coming our way. We must have figured the sky was getting dark with the passage of time, if we noticed at all. The rain shocked us, as the arrival of rain often did in our area. But it was always a pleasant surprise.

"Those aren't your tears?" Cal joked.

We looked up and had a choice.

We decided to go to his place.

I had those ten minutes during the drive for my doubts to inflate.

Kissing fully clothed in a public place was one thing. I hadn't dared to look at myself naked in years. I considered a U-turn every thirty seconds. I must have slowed down subconsciously, as a car was able to pull in between us from a side street, then another one passed me and the other car and cut in behind Cal's truck. The growing distance between me and Cal created a sense of dread that outweighed the thought of revealing my body to him, so I forged ahead. I told myself he was probably feeling something similar, as he wasn't exactly in playing shape. But he was a man, and men tend to think as long as their dick is visible and not laughably small, nobody will notice anything else.

The rain stopped, and the little drops of water on my hood merged into larger ones that jiggled with the vibration of the engine and the forward motion. I thought of my thighs.

I help up my phone and spoke into the text messenger.

"I can't. I'm fat."

I glanced at the words and felt my muscles prepare to turn. Again I resisted, but my finger brushed against the send icon before it reached the home button. I cursed out loud as the message was sucked into space with a whooshing sound effect.

A reply came back within seconds.

"You can. You're beautiful."

It felt like making out with him again.

"Stop texting while driving," I wrote him back.

"I hope you're not this bossy in bed," he replied.

His confidence buckled alongside mine, though, when we found ourselves facing one another in his barren living room with the lone futon and the high ceiling. The rain returned and pelted the thin walls. The echo was loud enough that we would not have been able to hear each other if we weren't so close.

"You're my first visitor," he said.

His uncertainty was endearing.

We kissed, but our lips were stalling, afraid to ask questions we both had.

"Funny," I said as we paused. "I felt more open in the parking lot."

"That's one of the things in my marriage I haven't admitted to you," he said. "Performance anxiety."

"It's clearly not a physical problem," I ran my hand up the front of his pants.

"No," he chuckled. "All mental. News flash."

"Commitment?"

"With my wife," he nodded. "Can you believe it?"

"Yes. Based on your fear of losing them."

"That, plus you're not the only one who feels fat."

I lassoed him with my arms.

"Thank you," I breathed into his chest. "I've got some fears about sex, too. But with Mike, it's fear of experimentation."

"He won't?"

"I won't."

"And I'm supposed to cure that?"

"Easier to cure than commitment issues."

We laughed softly.

I reared back and looked at him with the most straight face I could manage.

"Robot?" I asked. "Or not?"

We regained our appetite for each other and wound up on the futon. His mouth and the sound of the rain turning the house into a snare drum played by the forces of nature had me delirious. I could have been any age, at any point in time, any place.

I was on my back when he unlocked himself from our embrace and started kissing his way down my chest. His warm breath blew through the fabric of my shirt onto my breasts and kept me in flight. I landed back on earth when he reached my belly. It looked like I was pregnant, and he was kissing the baby inside.

I laughed, and when he asked me why, I told him what I was thinking.

"At least you can imagine a good reason for your belly," he said as he crawled back up next to me. "Mine offers no fantasies."

He gave me a small, sweet kiss and we took a breather. We stared up at the ceiling with the drumroll being played on it by the rain.

"Maybe it's best we stopped," I finally said.

He remained silent for a few beats longer than was comfortable, but then said something wonderful.

"What if we shared our stories instead?"

I can't imagine being any happier about anything else he could have said.

"Seriously?"

"One condition."

"Oh boy..."

"They have to be real," he caught my hesitation and tossed it aside. "As real as they can be."

"Of course."

"No. I mean it."

"I wouldn't have it any other way."

"We can't make anything up."

I saw what he was getting at.

"Only share what you honestly remember," he looked at me sternly, as though I was squirming.

"Is that possible?" I asked.

"It may make for a brief story."

"How can we even know?"

"We're going to try."

I quieted down and looked up at the noisy ceiling again. He probably thought I was bowing out or sulking. But I was thinking back as best I could to the day my life changed. I wanted the real thing for myself as much as him.

I started to doubt almost everything I had told everyone else. I went through my usual version, the one I had arrived at after many performances, and found myself swatting away nearly every scene. They were too clean, too clear, flowed too well. They seemed written rather than lived.

"All I have is the smell," I said at last. "I can't even hear the door shut behind us. He must have done it quietly. I don't think he turned off the lights, but that's the story I've created. I didn't want to see anything. I turned off my own lights. I've got his breath, though. That smell is hitting me hard. It's bad breath caused by stress, with a layer of breath mint. He knew he was going to do something wrong. He planned it, it made him nervous. He could taste the tension, so he tried to cover it up with a mint. But it was too far down inside of him. What he was going to do went way beyond his mouth. Did he think I would enjoy it if his breath was fresh? Maybe it was more for himself. If he could make his stress breath go away, it would feel better, like it was okay after all. Not that he kissed me. Or tried to. I would have remembered that. It would have seemed so ridiculous. 'Oh, okay. As long as you kiss me, go right ahead.' I know what he did. What he ended up doing after I locked in on that smell. But only because of the doctor's exam and the report afterwards. I don't remember any of it happening."

I turned to look at Cal. He had been looking up along with me, and still was.

"If I'm being honest," I said.

He turned my way and kissed me.

"For me, it's touch," he said. "There's a feeling I remember."

We looked back up at the ceiling, as though it was a screen that was reflecting our stories.

"The lower half of my face was the only part of my body that was exposed," he continued, "on the only day I can remember with any honesty. Sometimes even that part of me was covered if there was a dust storm. I felt like one of those sand people from Star Wars. But on that day, my nose and mouth were free. Maybe the weather was okay. Maybe I just needed a breather. Maybe I was about to tell a joke to break up the monotony. So much of what we did was so boring. We must have been doing something that wasn't considered dangerous, otherwise I never would have thought of saying anything, much less a joke, even when looking back. And it was surprising when it happened, when pieces of my friend landed on my lips and cheeks. I knew it was him. He usually ended up on my right somehow. On patrol, fixing something, digging something, there he was. I didn't notice the pattern until the explosion on my right. There was a noise I've never been able to imitate, and a vibration that came up through the ground and rattled my body, like some force from hell fighting its way out. No visual. The feeling of his blood and tissue on the only part of my body that was exposed wiped out any chance of that. It was going to be all about a feeling from that point on. When things settled down, we found out he was the only one killed, so that's how I knew it was him. He was the one stuck to me. That's how I know."

Cal paused for a while. I wasn't sure if he was done. I waited for him to let me know.

"I call him my friend," he said. "But I'm not sure if that's the right word. I don't know if we would have seen much of each other if he had lived. Probably not. We were close. We all were. I guess that's why we call each other 'brother'. We're forever connected to someone we might not hang out with if we had the choice."

The pause was longer this time.

I turned onto my side facing him, draped my arm across his chest, and threw my leg over both of his.

"Thank you," I told him.

"It felt good," he admitted.

"Because you didn't use protection."

He liked that.

I wouldn't have remembered that line if he hadn't liked it.

Our pillow talk switched to romantic comedies, and whether we could be subject of one.

"We come from different worlds," I said. "They always come from different worlds."

"We've got that going for us."

"We're not the physical types."

"Nobody is the physical type of the person who plays them in the movie," he said.

"We're casting this thing?"

"I'm including the movie we play inside our heads. The one we're always the hero of."

"Neither of us have an adorable pet," I added. "An animal that cuddles at just the right time, or covers its eyes when the couple kisses."

"I have an adorable kid."

"Then you've got it covered. But we're having an affair."

"So?"

I glanced at him.

"I don't mean 'so', as in having an affair isn't a big deal," he explained. "I mean it's pretty standard stuff in movies. At least one of them is involved with the wrong person."

"A fiancée," I corrected him. "Or serious boyfriend or girlfriend. Not a spouse. Breaking up a wedding can be funny. Breaking up a household…"

I left it at that.

He held me closer and exhaled.

"That's a different movie," he said toward the end of his breath.

"If you were a single dad, we could get this script approved," I said.

His exhale changed into something like a laugh.

"But our careers," he said. "Combat and a mental hospital."

"Not exactly rom com safe."

"Not exactly an advertising firm and a law office."

"Or a journalist and a really rich business person."

"A beauty and a beast."

I glared at him.

"Oh, you're the beauty," he caught my look. "Want to know why?"

"Oh," I kidded. "It's more than physical?"

"Way more."

I propped myself up on my elbow, and gestured for him to proceed.

"You got me to talk," he said.

He leaned over and kissed me.

"My wife is more the 'get over it' type," he added. "Of course, I might have played some part in that."

Then he kissed me again.

"Thank you," he whispered.

I thought about our trauma. How it may not work for a romantic comedy, but how much actors could play it up and win an award. Our characters would quiver in corners, yell at one another, end almost every scene in tears. But we would get better. The power of love would pull us through. We would wind up on a bicycle. I would ride on the handlebars while Cal would pedal and steer. It would be in autumn, so the leaves could make the moment really pop. And if the scene wasn't actually filmed in autumn, the leaves would be painted bright yellow and red.

The ceiling quieted down. The rain moved on like a date lurking impatiently by the door, letting me know it was time to go, to take advantage of the clear sky.

We made out for another decade until I unfastened myself from him, and only a few minutes had passed. Our hands glided down each other's arms as I rose from the futon until our fingers locked for a moment before letting go. We didn't say goodbye. I looked at him as long as I could without bumping into anything or tripping.

When I made it to the door he reached for his phone. He tapped it a couple of times and put it on the pillow next to his ear. I assumed it was music. I was curious what he was listening to. Something was on the screen, but I couldn't hear anything. I didn't want to backtrack and snoop. He saw me squinting by the door.

"Family cat," he held up the phone.

"Oh."

"It's a video of him purring. My daughter took it. I have it on a one-hour loop. Very relaxing."

"So you do have the adorable animal after all."

"He doesn't react to much. And he's not much of a lap cat."

I nearly re-used the line about how much more convenient it would be if he was a single guy with a pet, with a daughter, with a past. What a better fit that would be. But I just said goodnight, and thought about that bike ride down the tree-lined street in fall. The yellow and red leaves were a pretty picture, but they were also a countdown.

CHAPTER X

Our trance lasted a month. I would have liked more, but at least it was a month that was thirty-one days long.

We never did have sex. I would have remembered. It was a technicality. We did everything else. We were like a couple of evangelical teenagers trying to keep the promise of our promise rings. I think we always stopped ourselves so we could claim we didn't really have an affair. As an added bonus, I don't have to try and describe sex. That wasn't a factor in our decision at the time. I couldn't have known I was going to write about us. But I'm still grateful. I would be terrible at it, either too mechanical or too corny. The other stuff we did would be easier to describe than intercourse. The penetration is the tricky part, trying to say something besides "entered", "inserted", or "slid". But the other stuff still involves our bodies. Portraying us honestly, I would go for laughs, because if I take seriously our bellies and thighs and upper arms, I'm afraid I would turn people off. But going for laughs would be unjust, because it felt so good. It wasn't funny at all. Plus I can't make a decision about body parts. Penis sounds like a textbook, cock like a porno. Vagina and pussy are even farther apart. Maybe I could try it in another language. I could brush up on my Spanish, but I have a strong childhood connection to the dirty words. I would have to learn a whole new language, or invent a whole new sexual vocabulary. I would need a clean slate to write graphic sex.

We still used the term "do it". He would call and ask if I wanted to do it in one of the damaged, empty houses he was prepping, in every type of room marked by all manner of destruction. A dining room with water damage from an overflowing toilet, a bedroom with a hole in the ceiling from a fallen tree branch, a living room battered by a crashed party.

It was safer to do it in the mangled houses rather than a hotel room or a car parked in some remote but public place. As much as some of the older folks complained about our town getting too big, it was still too small for anyone looking to hide. The broken homes offered plenty of privacy and space, depending on the extent of the damage.

"Doing it" continued to include sharing another memory after we were done physically exhausting ourselves. We tried to keep the memories light, since we had started with our most disturbing. We did "earliest memory", "most embarrassing memory", "most random memory that has no significance but it's stuck there anyway for some reason", and found that we could recall more details when it came to carefree memories.

We went on something resembling a date once. Mike was under the weather and couldn't drive the seniors to the city for an art exhibit. I drove for him and invited Cal along as my friend, the substitute chaperone.

It was a beautiful day, twelve hours of foreplay. On the drive we talked as we always had, but with the knowledge of what it felt like to be wrapped around each other. In the museum we would put ourselves in the middle of a crowd huddled in front of a painting and see how much we could touch one another, and where, without being caught. We were still quite attentive to the seniors, because it was a turn-on to see the one you love being so kind to the people who are in your care.

We took a selfie together in front of the museum before I went to fetch the bus. A couple of the seniors photo-bombed us, a man and a woman whose energy I always admired. They were like young people in age makeup. The four of us laughed at the picture. It was actually a good one of me and Cal. If we ended up together for decades, it would be one of our favorites.

As long a day as it was, we still wanted each other after we dropped off the residents. I parked the bus behind the other bus in the rear lot of Mentor Manor, and we did it fully clothed in the back row of seats until we fell asleep mid-kiss.

I don't know who fell asleep first, but I know Cal woke up before me. He shook me awake. He wanted to make sure I got home not too long after we had parked the bus.

"Mike won't check," I stretched, yawned and scratched my way back into the present, wherever and whenever that was.

"It may come up in a conversation he has with someone who works here."

"He won't know what time I get home. He'll be asleep."

"I'm only looking out for you."

I remembered the selfie we took earlier in front of the museum. I checked my back pocket and my phone wasn't there. I panicked for a second, then saw it off to our side, stuck in the corner of the back seat, caught in the glow of a street light shining through the window. I reached for it and tapped my way to the picture of us. It made me smile.

He leaned over to see what I was smiling at.

"That's a great shot," he said.

"It is."

I took a deep breath and pressed the little picture of the garbage can beneath it. I was asked in writing if I wanted to delete the photo.

Cal and I looked at each other.

"We're not home wreckers," I smiled.

He smiled back.

I deleted our photo.

He held me and we sat quietly for a while.

"We repair homes," Cal finally said.

"We just clean them," I figured he was joking. "Well, you do. Then I come in and we mess around."

"Then you repair them."

I realized he was serious. But I didn't understand what he was saying.

He sat up and looked down the aisle.

"This may sound weird," he concentrated. "It's supposed to be a compliment. But since I've been with you, I've never felt more comfortable with my family."

I straightened up and looked down the aisle along with him.

"I see."

"You're hurt. Damn"

"No..."

"But?"

"Eh. Maybe."

"I'm sorry," he rubbed his face. "Never thought I'd be the one to start a fight by not keeping my mouth shut."

"Just another great effect I have on you."

"It's true," he looked at me. "So true."

He kissed me.

Our daydreams were leaking. We always knew we had nowhere to land them, but the sailing was always smooth. Reality was seeping through. I kissed him back and plugged the hole, but the puddle was still there.

Not that I didn't see his point. I saw perfectly.

My relationship with Mike and Zola had never felt better. I don't know if it actually was better, but I had more energy and patience with them than I could ever recall having. Things with Cheyenne seemed better, too, and that was a much higher standard. In spite of our bickering, we had always been a good pair. It helped that I looked good compared to her father, with his absence and steady stream of personal implosions. Things with Mike were destined to be forced. Even more so with Zola. So the new feelings of comfort I had with them were all the more fascinating.

I even asked for Zola's help when another hole of reality poked through our hull.

After agreeing to meet Cal in a house that had been blown in half by a gas leak while the family was out of town, I decided to kind of tell Cal I loved him by typing "love you" at the end of my text.

I went with "love you" rather than "I love you" because I figured keeping me out of it would be a softer sell. I almost went with "love ya," but felt too old to be deliberately misspelling words in a text.

Cal replied with "Live you too."

I assumed it was a typo, or autocorrect error, since the "i" and "o" are right next to each other on the keypad. I thought there was something accidentally profound about it, too. Live and love, so close together, just a letter away.

I kept this in mind when it happened again. We had done it in the half-collapsed house, and I texted him on the way home to say I had a wonderful time. I signed off with "love you", and he wrote back with another "live you".

It bothered me enough to consult Zola. I needed to know if there was more to the word switch than fat fingertips or AutoCorrect.

"Why do you ask?" Zola said from the fetal position on her bed, face buried in her phone screen.

"A friend from sewing class," I had my story planned out. "She and I got rather close, so I've been signing off with love and she's been coming back with live."

"Is she gay?"

"What?"

"Lesbian."

"I know. No."

"Maybe she thinks you are."

"Why?"

"Because that's the word people use when they're trying to figure out if they want to take the next step."

"Really?"

"Look it up in the urban dictionary."

"Is that online?"

She bothered to look at me for an irritated moment before resting her head back on her ear and educating me.

"Telling someone you live them is like saying you really like them, and want to spend time with them, but not as lovers."

I didn't want to ask Cal about it. I wanted to fend off reality as long as possible. When it was no longer fun, we would be done. I knew that from the moment we sacrificed our friendship for our bodies. Showing signs of insecurity would shorten the time we bought.

Besides, pettiness was starting to find us often enough without any needy questions from me.

He started getting picky about some of my mannerisms. He started small, noticing how I liked to chew with my mouth open for the first couple of bites when I ate something crispy.

I admit, I like the sound. Especially an apple.

Then he graduated. He said I always managed to come up with a personal example of my own when someone was sharing something that happened to them.

"That's like what happened to me," he accused me of saying, in so many words, so many times. Then I would tell my version.

"Which isn't always exactly like what happened to them," he said. "In fact, sometimes it's a real stretch."

I hoped that wasn't true.

I told him he only thought that because of our situation, where we did have something in common. He said I did it with everyone. Ours happened to be more intense than the average memory.

"I play a game with myself" he said. "I'll bring up a topic, and wait for you to jump in with your personal connection to it. Or when someone else is talking, I'll try to figure out when you're going to pounce. Then when you do, I try to figure out how much of your story is legit, and which parts are, well...not."

"Assuming I have a story."

"You always do," he smiled.

Maybe he thought he was being funny. That's why he smiled. Maybe he wasn't trying to be mean. But it hurt. I fretted over whether it was true. I had always taken pride in getting people to talk, at imagining myself hosting that talk show. Sure, I used my own stories to encourage them at times. Was it really all the time?

Then he said I stated the obvious too often.

"Yes, It's cold," he chuckled. "And sometimes it's hot. When a bad thing happens, it is bad, and hard to understand. Cute things are cute. No announcement needed."

He was smiling again, so I tried to be a good sport.

"What am I supposed to say when a cute dog runs up to me?" I asked.

"Say hello. Same thing with a cute kid. Talk to them. They like that. And Lord knows you like to talk. Would you want someone to start a conversation by commenting out loud about your looks?"

"If they commented out loud about my looks, we wouldn't be able to have a conversation."

"You know what I mean," he said. "And stop selling yourself short."

He didn't pick up on any irony about complimenting me in the process of criticizing me.

"And when we're on our phones or listening to the radio," I said, "and something awful comes across the news, I can't say how awful it is?"

"When are we ever on our phones when we're together?"

He rubbed my thigh and leaned in for a kiss.

I kissed him back, but he could tell I did it out of obligation.

He laughed into a defense.

"Narration doesn't add anything," he said.

I defended myself by claiming I use the narration as a lead-in to a discussion. Jumping right into a conversation can be awkward. Stating the obvious is a good way to get at what's underneath.

But I didn't voice that defense. My mind held onto it. I didn't want to argue. I only had so much energy I could devote to the time we had. I didn't want to spend it on conflict.

I should have been grateful. He was giving me excuses to bail out. He may have been doing it on purpose. What bothered him about me were the kinds of things you don't notice if you're planning on being with someone a long time. Or if you do notice them, you find them endearing because of who's doing them. Or you learn to ignore those things.

He may have been carving out his own escape hatch.

I asked what he meant by "live you".

He didn't know what I was talking about.

I showed him the texts.

"Nothing," he laughed.

He was laughing about a lot of things concerning me.

I told him about the urban dictionary definition.

"Like I'm hip enough to know that?"

He had a point.

"It's just big, dry fingers on a small keypad," he added.

But he didn't correct himself. He didn't say "love you".

It became a running joke between us. It always came from his direction.

We were becoming typical.

I was starting to feel like I had in any other relationship.

Except with Mike. Nothing faded with Mike. There were no heights to fall from. I started to feel guilty around him and Zola, instead of energized. I treated them the way I felt Cal was treating me. Only I wasn't doing a good job of smiling when I did so.

Doing it with Cal still felt great.

The feel of him made the annoying moments vanish.

I put a twist on our memory exchange after we had done it in a house that had been rented to some meth cookers for a year by some very absentee landlords. Cal was patching holes in the wall.

After we did it, and we were sprawled naked on a couch that was destined for an incinerator, I asked him to focus on the future instead. I asked him to make a prediction, or question what's to come.

"But nothing about us," I qualified. "We already know where this is headed."

"We do?"

"We're not giving up our families, so what choice do we have?"

"We can have it all," he announced, arms spread, gesturing across the filthy living room.

"Just answer the question," I shoved him.

"Stop," he fended me off. "You're making us jiggle."

"We jiggle when we're doing it."

"I keep my eyes closed."

"I'll do more than jiggle that ass," I playfully threatened him. "Come on now, look to the future."

He leaned back and took a deep breath.

"I wonder if I'm ever going to visit old battlefields," he said. "And old enemies. I see these feel-good stories once in a while, toward the end of a news broadcast, or on some weekend report. Used to be World War II vets visiting Normandy. Now it's Vietnam vets. They send an old dude over to some village where he was in some wicked firefight. Then they bring in some old Vietnamese guy who was in the VC, from the same fight. They shake hands, have a simple conversation through a translator, walk around the village, maybe have lunch, and the reporter does a voice over about how we're all human, the insanity of war, that kind of stuff. I have a hard time believing me or anyone I know is going to do that. I can't see any of us as one of those old dudes, going over to Herat and getting a guided tour of the town with an old Taliban. Maybe it's too soon. A lot can change, I suppose."

"I hope it does," I kissed the top of his head. "I'd like to watch that. I'll be sitting on my couch watching TV and there you'll be. I just won't be able to tell anyone I know you."

"You can tell them I'm an old friend."

We both smiled.

"That's sweet," I said.

"But wrong?" he heard something in my voice.

"We stopped being friends when you went down on me. If we ever were."

I wondered if I was trying too hard to get a little revenge over the little smears that had started to build. But I do believe in the separation of friends and lovers. If it was a return slap, it was grounded in a sincere conviction.

"I must confess," he said. "I cringe a bit when people say they married their best friend."

I crawled on top of him.

We kissed until we nearly broke our vow of chastity.

"I thought we weren't supposed to talk about us," he reminded me. "Your rule."

"Sorry. I just find us very interesting."

"We're not such a strange couple after all."

We cuddled as though we had finished having sex.

"Thank you for holding off my invisibility," I said.

"You're welcome?"

"I was reaching a point where I could test myself, test the world I live in, more like. I could stare at men for several minutes without them noticing. I could go on a crime spree without getting caught, if it weren't for the fact that women still see me. The older ones."

"I'm just one man."

"Which doubles my number."

I kissed him.

"For now," I added.

"That's your prediction," he caught on. "Your vision of the future."

I kissed him one last time.

"Thank you for noticing."

CHAPTER XI

I heard from Hannah that Cal and I were done.

She didn't say so exactly. She didn't even know she did. She didn't know Cal and I had been anything more than sewing class alumni.

I ran into her in the shampoo aisle in the box store at the edge of town, where all the other box stores loomed. She told me Cal had come into her family's restaurant with his wife and daughter.

It may have been coincidence. I may have been too self-absorbed. He just wanted to take them there. It was not a message that may get back to me. It was lunch at a great restaurant.

Hannah was excited about them being together. I think I did a good job of acting like her. But I could only perform for so long, so I changed the subject and asked her about costumes and conventions, and her plans for them.

I watched Cal's homecoming video online again. I needed to remind myself how good it was that they were together. I reached the part of the video I never paid attention to, the ending where the camera accidentally stays on for several extra seconds. I always wondered why they kept that part in, why nobody cut that ending before posting it.

Maybe because Cal's wife is in the shot. She glances into the lens for a couple of seconds as it holds steady just before the voice says "oops" and stops recording. I had a hunch just before I saw her. I suddenly recalled a vision of a woman being in the frame. And when she appeared, I figured it had to be her. There would be no reason to keep those extra seconds for the sake of a random bystander.

I replayed the final seconds for hours.

His wife was so much prettier than me. Even if she had gained weight since then, or wasn't putting herself together as carefully as she did for the homecoming, she had me beaten. She was a natural beauty. If I had only seen her in silhouette for those seconds, I would still be able to tell because of the way she carried herself. She moved like someone who was used to people paying attention to her, and was comfortable with it. She didn't try to grab the spotlight. She knew it would reach her eventually. She was unlike me in every way.

I realized I didn't know her name. Cal never offered it. I never asked.

I texted him.

"What's her name?"

He took a long time to reply. I imagined they were spending more time together.

He asked me to meet him the next day at our favorite lunch spot in the countryside, the one where we felt so far away.

He was sitting in his truck when I arrived, in the dirt parking lot where our footprints used to be. His window was rolled down and he was listening to angry talk radio.

"I'm studying," he explained while not quite looking at me. "My father-in-law is visiting next week. I want to know what he's going to be complaining about."

"Does he like Vietnamese food?"

He committed to looking at me.

"No."

We kept quiet for a while, mostly looking down.

"Should we bother going in?" I asked.

"Are you hungry?"

"Not anymore."

The quiet came back. We looked down on it some more.

"I love you," he said.

He used the "I". He beat me to it.

I cried.

Maybe for a minute. But much like when we kissed, it seemed much longer.

It was longer than I would have liked to cry. The difference was a matter of seconds, but those seconds swallowed me whole.

He said something else. Something about how he wasn't prepared to fall in love with me, but wasn't prepared to leave his family.

He wanted to explain himself. But he didn't have to. It was like trying to explain a joke. I got it. And if I didn't, the explanation wasn't going to help.

I said "I love you too."

I finally put myself into the sentence.

The first and last time.

As I walked back to my car, I heard him leave. The dust kicked up by his truck floated around me and escorted me the rest of the way. I tried not to breathe it in. I didn't see any of it on me as I sat in my car. There was nothing to dust off. But it was there. I ran my fingers through my hair and it felt coarse. I smelled dry earth.

I didn't start the car for a while. I didn't want to pull up next to him at a stop light once we were back in town. I waited until I figured he would have reached his destination. I sat there and remembered an article I read in school, or at work, or on my phone. The point was that love is an accommodation. We give people we love what they need. I liked it at the time because it helped me feel good about being with Mike. But it worked for Cal and me, too. He needed to be with his family as much as I needed to be with mine. We loved each other, so we let that happen. We weren't possessive, we weren't jealous. We were accommodating. I was proud of us.

But I was sad.

I didn't cry over him ever again. It wasn't that kind of sad. It was always going to be there, humming underneath my life like a heartbeat. I could feel it, but not touch it, not see it. And even a picture of it, an x-ray, isn't really the thing itself.

We didn't keep in touch.

I would drive by his house every so often. It was a busy street, a main artery through town, so it was easy to pass without feeling pathetic. I never saw him, just his truck. A few months after we left one another in the dust, his truck no longer appeared in the driveway.

I found a Facebook page his wife had started. It was kind of a fan page for people who had seen the video. I was able to view it without liking it or joining it. She announced they had moved to Los Angeles. Cal had been offered a job at the VA office down there. I scrolled back through the posts that covered the time they were split. There weren't many of them. She didn't have to say much. Plenty of people posted messages. Every few weeks she left a quick note thanking everyone for their kind words and offering an update on how their daughter was doing in school and in dance class. It was easy enough to stay focused on their daughter. She was the star of the show, like Cal said. No need for his wife to share any details about their marriage. That's not what people came for.

I scrolled back up to the Los Angeles announcement. She posted a photo of them standing in front of a little house in a very suburban neighborhood. They were standing diagonally from the house on the front lawn, so you could not only see their house, but several more houses down the street. At the end of the block stood a large office building, hundreds of feet high. It looked like a space ship that had landed to study humans in their preferred habitat.

The more time passed, the less I visited the page. I had kids of my own to focus on.

Cheyenne had a baby with Augie.

When she told me she was due, I didn't have to act happy, like I thought I would. She was so overjoyed, I just rode her happiness.

It was another girl. Cheyenne named her Lakota.

One day a few months past her first birthday, I was watching her stagger around the playground in the park. Zola was sitting next to me.

"I wonder if she'll break the cycle in your family," Zola said.

"What cycle?"

"Teen pregnancy."

I playfully slapped her arm.

"Cheyenne was twenty when she had Lakota," I reminded her.

"But she was nineteen when she got pregnant."

"Barely."

"Like there's a huge difference between nineteen and twenty," Zola scoffed.

"Maybe not," I said. "But there's a huge difference between nineteen and sixteen."

"Fair enough," Zola said. "But tell me you wouldn't have rather had her wait."

"It's not so much the age as it is the father," I confided in her.

Zola and I started to get along after she entered high school. Her world got bigger. She could make a friend or two and blend into the crowd.

She smiled.

"Augie's not that bad," she said.

"There are worse," I agreed.

We watched Lakota put her hands on the bottom of the slide and look up the chute. She turned and squeaked at us, then moved on.

I was sitting watching a child again, as I suspected I would end up doing all along.

I wondered if Cal was doing the same.

His daughter would be too old for this sort of thing. But maybe they had another one. Or he could be watching his oldest daughter's dance recital or soccer game, or some other activity that's only interesting if your child is involved.

His wife's Facebook page had become pretty much inactive. I wasn't the only one who stopped visiting. An occasional message trickled in every month or so, according to the time stamps. She never posted anything anymore. I took this as a good sign. The cute girl had grown, the novelty had worn off, other videos moved ahead of theirs on the viral pecking order. They were a normal family now. I hoped that was good enough for them.

On the job I knew a psychiatrist who told me about the "one-year rebound," as she liked to call it. She would deal with families who were hurt by one of our patients, or hurt that one of our patients was part of their family. She said after a major event in life, happy or sad, about a year later most of us become the same person we were before it happened. We are the sum of memories we don't remember very well.

I was confident I had been like most people when it came to the attack. Despite occasional flashbacks, I was for the most part the same person I was before, even more so. I was once again flattering myself into thinking I could help people, eager to talk, perhaps combining those two things too often.

When it comes to Cal, I'm not sure if I've rebounded quite the same way. I wonder too often if it meant as much to him as it did to me. I search my memory for clues about his thoughts more than my own. Not that I can ever really know, even if we got in touch and he told me.

I find myself staring at something but seeing nothing while I run an errand or watch my granddaughter. I hang out with Hannah or Laurie and it happens again. We have a great time, but they remind me of Cal, so I stare ahead as if it will help me look back.

I remind myself to feel grateful for normalcy. I think of all the miserable situations I could be in. I live like royalty compared to most of the world.

Still I stare.

Mike offers calm, but not understanding. I'm not sure anyone can. I'm not sure I want to be known that well for that long. I'll need some secrets.

I think of the photo we took, that selfie in front of the museum with the residents twice our age beaming behind us. We deleted it, but I imagine it's still out there, floating inside the wires of a huge computer in a massive building that belongs to an enormous company. It's not a photo anymore. It's a bunch of numbers. When the numbers line up, we appear.

I'll remember things differently in the future. I might want to.

I might need to.

We're not cameras.

We're not robots.

Also by Sean Boling

The Current Mr. Orr
Devin's Best Afterlife
Once in Two Lifetimes
Revenge and Wellness in the Sweet Hereafter

Standalone
Cut Flowers
Abraham the Anchor Baby Terrorist
Pigs and Other Living Things
The Summer of Our Foreclosure
Satellite Campus
A Charter to That Other Place
The Latest Version of My Love Story
Show Them What They Won
The Name Field
Should
Moral Adjacent
Over Here We Have

About the Author

Sean lives with his family in Templeton, California. He teaches English at Cuesta College.

www.ingramcontent.com/pod-product-compliance
Lightning Source LLC
Chambersburg PA
CBHW020530160726
47992CB00005BA/2330